He nodded. ' mind at ease. ... tention of being a part of Samantha's life.'

Relief swept through Katrina, unknotting muscles she hadn't even known she'd been holding tight. 'That's great.'

Alex stared at her, face expressionless. For some reason she began to feel uneasy, a restless sensation attacking the base of her spine.

'So, we're in agreement, then?' he asked. 'We have to do what's best for Samantha?'

There was an odd note in Alex's voice she couldn't quite decipher. It made her unease quickly expand into out-and-out wariness. 'Of course. That's why I came back.'

'Good,' Alex said, breaking into her thoughts. 'Then the only logical course of action is for the two of you to move in with me.'

Katrina blinked. Dragged in a breath. Blinked again. Surely she hadn't heard him right? Because she thought he'd just said… Well, she thought he'd just said… She shook her head.

'I insist.' His tone was smooth, but underlined by steel.

Tina Duncan lives in trendy inner-city Sydney with her partner, Edy. With a background in marketing and event management, she now spends her days running a business with Edy. She's a multi-tasking expert. When she's not busy typing up quotes and processing invoices, she's writing. She loves being physically active, and enjoys tennis (both watching and playing), bushwalking and dancing. Spending quality time with her family and friends also rates high on her priority list. She has a weakness for good food and fine wine, and has a sweet tooth she has to keep under control.

HER SECRET,
HIS LOVE-CHILD

BY
TINA DUNCAN

First published in Great Britain 2010
Harlequin Mills & Boon Limited,
Eton House, 18-24 Paradise Road, Richmond, Surrey TW9 1SR

© Tina Duncan 2010

ISBN: 978 0 263 21326 3

Printed and bound in Great Britain
by CPI Antony Rowe, Chippenham, Wiltshire

HER SECRET,
HIS LOVE-CHILD

CHAPTER ONE

'"HELLO, Alex." Is that all you have to say to me after disappearing to God knows where for months on end?' Alex Webber demanded.

He regretted the words instantly, not only because he had an audience but because they also demonstrated a rare loss of control on his part.

But that was hardly surprising, was it? He'd been caught way off-guard by Katrina's sudden appearance. Bursting in on him uninvited was not her style at all but, more importantly, she'd been missing for months.

Katrina Ashby shrugged her shoulders, sending her caramel-blonde hair rippling around her leather-clad shoulders. 'I suppose I should have added, *how are you*?'

Alex clenched his hands into fists. Although he wasn't a violent man, and had never lifted a finger against a woman in his life, he wanted nothing more than to stride across the room and shake Katrina until her teeth rattled.

After all of this time, how dared she turn up like this, out of the blue, and say, 'Hello, Alex,' as if nothing had happened?

His insides contracted on a burst of anger as week

upon week of frustration imploded inside him. At the same time, other parts of him were swelling as another far more primitive form of frustration made itself known.

Forget shaking her until her teeth rattled, Alex conceded. What he really wanted to do—even though he shouldn't—was to pull her into his arms and kiss her until she wrapped her arms around his neck and sighed her surrender into his mouth.

Aware they had an interested audience—several board members were openly gawping, others surreptitiously looking backwards and forwards between them behind the cover of hands and folders—Alex did neither.

'Out!' he commanded.

Body rigid and teeth clenched, Alex remained where he was as the board, five men and two women, rose hastily to their feet and competed for who could reach the door first. They knew their boss well. He rarely lost his temper, but, when he did, it was usually a major eruption. Able to read the danger signs, each and every one of them was eager to get out of the firing line.

When the door closed behind them, Alex moved purposefully towards Katrina. She didn't back away from him. She stood her ground and gave him look for look, with a glint of challenge in her eyes he hadn't seen before.

'I asked you a question,' he asked silkily when he stopped in front of her.

She angled her chin into the air. 'And I answered you. Hello, Alex. How are you?'

'I'll tell you how I am.' He stepped closer until they were almost touching. He could smell the scent of her perfume—a gift he'd had his PA send her for her birthday shortly before she'd vanished—and could see the little specks of golden-brown in her cat-like green eyes. 'I'm furious!'

She cocked her head. 'Why?'

'Why?' Alex thought the top of his head might explode; he could actually feel the blood pumping at his temples. He grasped her shoulders and put his face close to hers. 'Because you disappeared without a trace, that's why!'

She smiled. 'Without a trace? Isn't that the name of an American TV show?'

'Katrina!'

Her smile faded. 'I didn't disappear, Alex. I just decided to go away for a while, that's all.'

Katrina had always been the cool, collected type—except when they'd been in bed together. Then she'd been wonderfully abandoned, returning kiss for kiss, touch for touch and pleasure for pleasure with a passionate intensity that blew his mind and everything else.

Normally, he liked the fact that she was so self-contained, but today her calm demeanour annoyed the hell out of him.

'Without telling me where you were going or how long you'd be gone for?' Alex prompted through gritted teeth.

'I told the people who mattered,' she said softly.

Alex exhaled sharply, his teeth snapping together. 'And you didn't consider including me in that group?'

Her gaze remained steady on his. 'No. I didn't.'

Alex struggled to keep his anger contained. He knew he was overreacting badly but he couldn't seem to help himself.

'Why not?' he bit out.

'Why should I tell you?' she shot back at him, that

new challenging light in her eyes making them appear greener than usual.

His fingers flexed, digging into the soft leather of her jacket. 'Because you owed it to me,' he grated, the answer dragged from somewhere deep inside him.

Alex wasn't sure what angered him more: the fact that she had run out on him, or that she was the one to have betrayed him.

Of all the women he'd been with over the years, Katrina was the last one he would have picked to put him in this position.

'*Owed it* to you?' Her eyes flashed like quick-silver and the tip of her index finger dug into the centre of his chest, as if she was trying to bore a hole through to the other side. 'I don't owe you a thing, Alex. Not a single thing. And don't you forget it!'

Alex was stunned by her reaction. The Katrina he'd known would never have spoken to him the way this Katrina just had.

Pressure built inside his head until once again Alex thought the top of his head might explode.

Dragging in a breath, he fought for control.

He hated losing his temper. It reminded him of his father's monstrous behaviour, and the last thing he ever planned on doing was following in James Webber's footsteps!

He pulled her closer. Their bodies brushed and a surge of electricity powered through him. 'You're wrong about that. You owe me, all right. We were lovers, damn it!'

'*Lovers?*' She barked out a laugh, but there was no amusement in it. 'Don't you mean I was your mistress?'

Although she'd never said so, Alex had sensed on

more than one occasion that Katrina hadn't been entirely happy with the role she'd played in his life. Like most women, she'd wanted a wedding ring and children, despite the fact he'd warned her up front that neither of those things was on offer.

They weren't on offer to any woman. And never would be.

'I'm not going to argue semantics with you. The point is we were together for almost a year. If that doesn't earn me the right to be told you were leaving Sydney, then what does?'

Katrina tried to shrug out from under his touch. When he refused to let her go she glared up at him. 'The operative word is *were*, Alex: we *were* lovers. We're not any more. The last time I saw you, you told me our relationship was over. Or have you forgotten that?'

'No, I haven't forgotten.'

He hadn't forgotten a thing.

Not what she tasted like.

Or smelled like.

Or how she looked when she fell apart in his arms.

And certainly not what she'd told him on that last fateful day they'd been together. Each and every word was indelibly carved into his brain as if someone had put them there with a hammer and chisel.

Releasing Katrina, Alex stalked to the window where he stood staring out at the Sydney skyline, fists shoved deep in his trouser pockets, tension drawing his shoulders up towards his ears.

'You had to know that wasn't the end of it,' he said quietly. 'You were pregnant, for goodness' sake!'

'What's that got to do with anything?' she asked,

still sounding as cool as a cucumber, her eyes boring a pair of twin holes between his shoulder blades.

'What has that got to do with anything…?' Alex spun around to face her, blue eyes wide and incredulous. His fists clenched and unclenched against the silk lining of his pockets. 'Did you really think you could drop that kind of bombshell and not expect me to contact you again?'

She cleared her throat, and for the first time since bursting unannounced into the boardroom she didn't look quite so sure of herself; the challenge in her eyes was replaced by uncertainty. 'I'm not sure what to say. You were so cold that day. I honestly thought I'd never see you again.'

'Of course I was cold. I was in shock, damn it!'

'And do you think I wasn't?' Katrina demanded, voice rising.

Her words hung in the air like the residue of rifle fire, bouncing off one wall and then another.

Her mouth twisted. 'Oh, that's right!' She slapped an open palm against the centre of her forehead. 'How could I forget? You claimed you weren't the father.'

She looked at him as if she half-expected him to contradict her.

Alex stared stonily back, his silence answering for him.

'How can you believe that? We made love all the time. I could have become pregnant on any of those occasions, and you know it.'

'Aren't you forgetting one little thing?' he asked, dangerously quiet.

'And that is?'

'Protection,' he issued in a hard voice. 'I took care

of our precautions. Too many women have tried to catch themselves a rich husband by getting pregnant deliberately.'

That was obviously what Katrina was trying to do. But what made it worse, so, so much worse, was that she was trying to do it with another man's child.

She had to be.

Because Alex had an even better reason than the precautions he'd just referred to for believing the child wasn't his—a reason that was so strong it put that belief almost beyond question.

Her treachery bit deep, gouging at him with hungry teeth.

It had been there like a thorn in his side, slowly leeching its poison into his system and raising all sorts of questions in his mind.

When she'd taken him to the heights of passion had it merely been a means to an end? Had she been there with him on the journey, feeling what he was feeling, or had she been putting on an act while her brain had clinically thought about her forthcoming plan?

The realisation that what he had thought was real and beautiful might just have been a sham left him feeling empty inside—and angry outside.

She gasped. 'Are you accusing me of being a gold-digger?'

He shrugged. 'If the shoe fits.'

'Well, the shoe doesn't fit. I wouldn't have you even if…even if…' She waved her hands through the air. 'Even if you were served up to me on a platter with a million-dollar cheque in your mouth!'

Alex laughed; he couldn't help it. The suggestion

was so ludicrous he couldn't believe she'd actually had the gall to make it.

She lunged at him, hand arcing through the air. 'You cold-hearted…!'

Alex caught her hand and forced it back to her side before pulling her close. He'd never seen her lose her temper before. Her eyes were glittering with emerald fire, streaks of colour striping razor-sharp cheek bones. An incredible energy was emanating from her, so powerful he felt he could reach out and touch it with his hands.

A surge of lust—a lust he knew he should not be feeling—sent his blood roaring through his veins. He put his face close to hers. 'Don't push me, Katrina. I'm *this* close—' he held up thumb and forefinger with barely a hair's breadth separating them '—to doing something we'll both regret.'

'Don't push you?' she shouted, eyes so wide they dominated her face. 'Are you out of your mind? It's the other way around—don't *you* push—'

Alex silenced her with his mouth.

He hadn't planned on doing it; it just happened.

He kissed her savagely, his mouth hard and uncompromising.

Katrina stiffened until it felt as if he was holding an ironing board in his arms; her hands were like steel braces pressing forcefully against his chest. Alex fed a hand into her hair and cupped the back of her head, the other clamping around her waist at the base of her spine.

She tasted sweet, like the nectar from sun-warmed peaches, and as intoxicating as the finest wine. Something stirred inside him, something he hadn't felt since he'd last been with her. Something that not one of the women he'd slept with in the last seven months had evoked in him.

His mouth softened on hers and he began kissing her as if those months had never existed. As if she'd never told him she was pregnant and he'd never told her it was over.

His head spun.

His body stirred.

He was rock hard in under three seconds flat.

Katrina was the only woman who'd ever been able to do that to him. After all this time, and everything that had happened between them, Alex hadn't expected her appeal to still be so strong. But her effect on him was as powerful as it had ever been, if not more so.

Heart pounding, he ran the tip of his tongue over her lower lip then nibbled on it with his teeth, his hands relaxing until he was cradling her against him.

And slowly, oh, so slowly, the resistance melted out of her body. She sighed, her hands clutching at his shirt front, her lips softly parting.

Then she began kissing him back.

His kisses grew hotter and more demanding, his lips devouring hers, his tongue thrusting into her mouth to savour her inner sweetness. Heat seeped into his bloodstream until he felt saturated with raw desire. The world spun out of control, taking his sanity with it.

He was vaguely thinking about locking the door and carrying her to the long boardroom-table when Katrina began pushing against his chest again.

'Stop it, Alex!' she gasped, dragging her mouth out from under his. She was breathing so fast she could barely get the words out. 'Stop it! I don't want this.'

Alex lifted his head and stared down at her.

Her eyes were wide, the golden-brown specks gleaming, her mouth moist and kiss-swollen. A hectic flush had coloured her cheekbones, and scented heat was radiating off her skin.

She looked the way she'd always looked when they made love, and the familiarity of it sent a wave of satisfaction through him.

'Yes, you do.' He smudged his thumb across her lower lip. 'Do you think I didn't notice the way your eyes ate me up when you burst in here? And just now you were with me kiss for kiss. You're hungry for me— go on, admit it.'

Alex wasn't quite sure why it was so important that she admit she still wanted him, but it was. Important enough that a clamouring sense of urgency to hear her say the words was rising up inside of him.

Katrina tore herself out of his arms and stalked across the room, putting the length of the boardroom table between them. 'That…that kiss was a mistake,' Katrina said, wringing her hands together in front of her as if wringing a tea towel she was trying to extract water from. 'It shouldn't have happened.'

Alex opened his mouth to challenge the truth of that statement but just as quickly closed it again.

Katrina was right.

It *was* over between them.

It had to be.

Why was he thinking any differently?

Because he wasn't thinking with the head, he admitted grudgingly.

He dragged in a breath. 'I couldn't agree more,' he replied coolly.

She blinked at him. 'You…you agree?'

He nodded. 'Of course. I kissed you merely because I was trying to prove a point.'

Her mouth compressed into a straight line. 'And what point is that?'

'You claimed you wouldn't take me even if I was served up to you on a platter,' he drawled softly, refusing to admit the comment had dented his ego. 'That kiss just proved you'd take me any way you can get me. Only I'm not buying.'

'Why you arrogant, egotistical playboy!' she spluttered, green eyes flashing fire at him. 'Might I remind you that I was the one who stopped just now, not you?'

Alex was once again surprised by her outburst. Katrina had lost her temper twice since she'd arrived, something he couldn't recollect her doing even once in the almost-twelve months he'd known her.

'I'm not going to debate that with you. Now, you obviously came here for a reason. Maybe it's time we stopped talking about the past and got to the point of this meeting. Because, frankly, I don't understand what you're doing here.'

A mixture of emotions flashed across her face so fast he couldn't register what each one was. Her breath hissed out of her mouth. Without another word, she spun on her heel and stalked towards the door.

Alex frowned. 'Come back here, Katrina. This meeting isn't over. It's not over until I say it's over.'

She threw him a scathing look over her shoulder and wrenched open the door, disappearing through it before he had a chance to stop her.

Alex lunged after her, then slowed when he heard the murmur of voices. He frowned. It sounded as if Katrina was talking to his PA, Justine.

He was at the door when he almost collided with Katrina, who was coming back into the room.

She was carrying something.

Alex looked down automatically.

He stiffened. The air locked tight in his lungs, his heart knocking against his breast bone as if it was trying to shatter it. His body moved from stiff to rigid in the blink of an eye, as if he'd just been spray-painted with quick-drying cement.

Staring up out of what he now realised was a carry cot was a tiny, gurgling baby.

He looked up. 'What the—?' Alex dragged in a ragged breath, his eyes narrowed on her face. 'I— You—' He snapped his mouth closed, dragged in another breath and then accused harshly, 'You had the baby!'

Katrina frowned. 'Of course I had the baby.' She looked down and her mouth softened. 'Meet your daughter. Her name is Samantha.'

Katrina had never seen Alex speechless before, but that was certainly what he was now. His sensual mouth was working but so far no sound had emerged. At least, nothing intelligible. His blue eyes were fixed with piercing intensity on their tiny daughter, as if he'd never seen a baby before.

'Well, aren't you going to say something?' she asked anxiously, her hands shaking so much she thought she might drop the cot and its precious contents.

Alex lifted his head slowly, his gaze refocussing on her. 'I didn't know you'd had the baby,' he said, sounding dazed.

Katrina frowned. She put the cot down on the end of the table before turning back to Alex. 'That's the second time you've said that. Of course I had the baby. Why are you so surprised?'

He blinked and the dazed look slowly cleared. 'When you disappeared the way you did, I presumed you'd decided to abort the child.'

'What…what did you say?' she asked in a voice that was little more than a whisper.

Alex shrugged. 'It was the only reason I could think of to explain why you packed up and left the way you did.'

'You have to be kidding?' Katrina burst out incredulously. She'd never lost her temper as many times as she had during this meeting. But she'd spent months stewing over the way Alex had treated her, and he was doing the same thing again now: pushing all of the right buttons to send her anger into overdrive. 'I can think of a dozen reasons, and not one of them would be *that*.'

'Then why?'

'You didn't think I might have needed a friend right about then?' When he stared at her blankly, she gritted her teeth. 'I was twenty-two, Alex. Pregnant and alone. The man I loved had just accused me of trying to foist another man's child on to him. What did you think I was going to do—carry on as if everything was normal?'

His mouth curled. 'You're not going to try that old chestnut, are you?'

She blinked at him. 'What old chestnut?'

He waved a hand. 'Love. You just said that you love me. This is the first I've heard of it.'

Her heart resounded in her chest with the same boom as rolling thunder. 'I said *loved*, Alex. Past tense. And I didn't tell you how I felt because it was clear you didn't love me. Or want my love.' She laughed harshly, mocking her feelings and the dream that one day he would love her in return. 'Don't worry. I realise now that it was all an illusion. The man I thought I loved didn't really exist. He was obviously just a figment of my imagination, because he would never have treated me the way you have.'

'And how have I treated you?' Alex demanded in a cool voice.

She wrung her hands together again. She'd been determined to keep calm during this meeting but her anxiety and distress were getting the better of her. 'For one, he would never have accused me of aborting our child without telling him!'

'I'm sorry,' Alex said stiffly. 'It sounded like the most logical explanation.'

'Well, it wasn't. I needed to be with someone who genuinely cared about me. Someone who would give me emotional support instead of blaming me for the situation, like you did.'

He frowned. 'So you went to stay with a friend?'

She nodded. 'Just for a couple of weeks. Until I found somewhere else to live.' She gave him the kind of look that could curdle milk. 'I had no intention of staying in an apartment being paid for by you. So much for your claim that I'm a gold-digger!'

His remark had been totally uncalled for. She hadn't been happy about him renting an apartment for her in the first place. It was only when Alex had explained that its location meant they could see more of each other that she'd given in.

Alex stared at her through narrowed eyes. 'What friend?'

She angled her chin upwards. 'I don't think that's any of your business, do you?'

His mouth hardened. 'Just tell me one thing.'

'And what's that?'

'Was it a man?'

'No, it wasn't a man. What makes you ask that?'

He shrugged. 'It makes sense.'

Katrina frowned. 'It might make sense to you, but it doesn't to me.'

His piercing blue eyes bored into hers. 'I would have thought it made perfect sense for you to stay with the father of your child for the duration of your pregnancy.'

She gasped and pressed a hand to her chest, where her heart was frantically beating. 'What did you say?'

Alex threw a cold glance at the cot. 'Whoever fathered that child, it wasn't me,' he said in a voice that rasped like sandpaper down her spine.

Katrina's stomach churned, her heart kicked, and it was all she could do to remain standing upright.

She was so angry and hurt that she wanted nothing more than to spin on her heel, stalk out the door and never see Alex again.

If it wasn't for Samantha, she would have done exactly that. But her daughter's needs had to come first—and she needed both of her parents.

'She *is* yours,' she finally gritted out.

'No. She's not. I always made sure we were protected.'

'Not always.'

'OK. So I forgot—once,' Alex dismissed.

She sucked in a lungful of much-needed air and glared at him. 'That's all it takes. Besides, all forms of contraception have a failure rate, including condoms. And, since I didn't sleep with anybody else, it's physically impossible for anyone else to be the father.'

Alex frowned. Katrina could tell by the way he was looking at her that the cogs of his mind were grinding as he assessed what she'd just said. Finally, face hardening, he said, 'I don't believe you. The child is not mine. And I will expect you to sign something attesting to that fact.'

Katrina folded her arms defiantly. 'I'm not signing anything.'

'Oh yes, you are. The document will list a number of conditions: one, you will never approach me regarding the child again. Two, you will never ask me for money. And three, you will never publicly try to claim I am the father of your child.'

Katrina was so stunned all she could do was stare and keep on staring.

'When the document is ready, you will sign it,' Alex continued in the same harsh voice.

Katrina surged to her feet, limbs shaking, hands clenched into fists. She'd never felt so insulted in her life—unless she counted his earlier accusation about secretly aborting their child!

Angry—furious, more like it—Katrina stared him in the eye and resisted the urge to smack him across his handsome face.

'*That* is not going to happen.'

Without saying another word, she scooped up the carry cot and stormed out of the boardroom.

CHAPTER TWO

ALEX frowned as he watched Katrina march out of the room. 'Katrina! Come back in here.'

Alex narrowed his eyes as he waited, in no doubt that she'd reappear at any moment. He'd always found her... Well, the truth was he'd always found her rather biddable. She'd always fallen in with his plans, even when he'd known she wasn't entirely happy with them. She'd always said yes, even if it had meant changing her schedule to fit in with his.

Put simply, like every other woman who'd shared his bed, she had never once said no to him.

Any minute now, she would reappear. He would re-iterate his intentions. She would leave...and it would all be over.

The thought should have pleased him. But somehow it didn't.

The thought of never seeing Katrina again, never tasting her again, left him feeling oddly unsettled, although he couldn't imagine why.

Forcing the thought aside, Alex scowled.

Realising that Katrina should have reappeared by now, he sprang towards the door.

A quick scan of Justine's private office showed no sign of either Katrina or the carry cot. He strode to Justine's desk. She was on the phone and acknowledged him with a slight smile and a raised eyebrow.

Too impatient to wait, Alex snatched the receiver out of her hand and dropped it unceremoniously into the cradle.

Justine gaped up at him. 'What did you do that for?'

Alex could understand her surprise. In the three years she'd worked for him, he'd never done such a thing. 'Where's Katrina?'

'She left.'

'What do you mean she left?' Alex roared, his insides contracting on a wave of frustration.

Justine blinked up at him. 'Well, she came out and said goodbye, and then she left.'

The words hit Alex in the centre of his back as he left the room and began sprinting down the corridor towards the lift. By the time it offloaded him in the vast foyer on the ground floor, there was no sign of her.

He raced to the exit and lost precious seconds waiting for the glass doors to slide open. Like the lift, they appeared to be moving in slow motion.

Out on the pavement, Alex looked left and right, then scanned the other side of the road.

There was no sign of Katrina.

Alex swore, astounded Katrina had run out on him for a second time. People just didn't do that to him.

Alex returned inside, stopping beside the security guard standing inside the doorway. His name tag read David Greenway.

'David, did you see an attractive woman come

through here a few minutes ago? She has caramel-blonde hair and green eyes. She was wearing a black leather jacket. You couldn't miss her.'

David Greenway's Adam's apple bobbed up and down as he swallowed. 'I'm sorry, sir. We get a lot of people through here.'

Alex clamped his teeth so tightly together he thought they might shatter. He was about to turn away when he thought of something. 'She was carrying a baby in a cot.'

'Ah.' The security guard nodded eagerly. 'Yes, I remember her now.'

'Did you see which way she went?'

David nodded. 'She flagged down a taxi virtually right outside the door.'

'Damn.' Alex stared down at the tips of his shiny black shoes and then up again. 'Did you see what company?'

'As it happens, I did. It was Lime Taxis.'

'Well done, David. Well done,' Alex said, patting him on the shoulder and hurrying away.

Back in his office Alex pressed the speed-dial button for the Royce Agency, the private-detective firm he'd engaged on numerous occasions to do background checks on prospective employees and upgrade the security in his homes and offices.

He'd also engaged the agency to find Katrina. It was the first time the outfit had failed him, which was why they had continued to search for her free of charge.

He was put through to Royce, the owner, straight away.

Briefly and concisely, Alex outlined what had happened.

'Lime Taxis, you said?' Royce confirmed. 'The information is going to cost you.'

'I don't care how much it costs,' Alex grated. 'Find her.'

He'd spent seven months kicking his heels, wondering where Katrina was and what she was doing.

His interest hadn't been in the least personal, of course. The minute he'd discovered she was trying to foist another man's child on him, he'd known their relationship was over. But he had felt it wise to keep an eye on her so that the situation didn't explode in his face.

But Katrina had hidden herself well. He had no intention of letting the same thing happen again; he wanted the experts on the job while her trail was still hot.

'OK,' Royce said. 'I'll call you back as soon as I have the information.'

'Make it fast.'

Alex paced his office like an animal trapped in a much-too-small cage. When his mobile phone rang, Alex almost broke the thing in his eagerness to answer. 'Royce?'

Royce got straight to the point. 'The taxi dropped her off at an apartment in Waverton. Here's the address.'

Alex scribbled the information down on his notepad. Before ending the call, he said, 'I want you to send someone over to the apartment to watch Katrina. They are not to let her out of their sight. I want to know where she goes and who she sees. And I want a report on who she's staying with. Got it?'

Alex didn't wait for a reply. Despite the fact Royce and his people had failed to find Katrina, they were still good operatives. The best, in fact. He had no doubt his request was already spinning into action.

Ripping the page from his notepad, Alex shoved it in his pocket and left the office.

'I'm going to be out for the rest of the day,' he said, striding past Justine's desk without pause.

'But you have appointments all afternoon,' Justine called after him.

'Cancel them,' Alex flung over his shoulder. 'I have more important things to attend to!'

Katrina was scrubbing the stove top when the doorbell rang. There was something therapeutic about making the white enamel gleam. She always cleaned when she was upset or had some serious thinking to do. And right at this moment she could tick the box against both of those things.

The doorbell pealed again.

'Coming,' she called, dropping her cloth then pulling off her green rubber-gloves and flinging them down on the edge of the kitchen sink.

Hurrying to the door, she pulled it open.

She was quite unprepared to find Alex standing on the doorstep.

For one stunned second all she could do was gape up at him like a stranded fish. Then she dragged in a breath, regathered her wits and tried to slam the door in his face.

She was too late.

An expensive black leather shoe wedged itself between the door and the jamb. Then a strong, long-fingered hand curled around the edge of the door and began pushing it open.

Katrina leant against it with all her weight, but it was useless. She was no match for Alex's size and strength. It was like an ant trying to push over an elephant.

Recognising that she was wasting her time, Katrina

stepped away from the door so fast that Alex practically fell into the apartment.

After staring at her long and hard, he looked around. 'You live *here*?'

The slight emphasis he'd given the last word managed to convey exactly what he thought of the apartment. Her hackles, which were already sticking up like the needles on a porcupine after their earlier meeting, bristled some more.

Katrina followed his gaze. She had to admit the carpet needed replacing. It was threadbare in places and stained in others. The walls were also long overdue for a coat of paint.

Peter had apologized for the condition of the unit, but he'd over-extended himself when he'd bought it and was struggling to meet the mortgage repayments.

Katrina had jokingly said it was OK because it didn't show up her furniture. It would be generous to call her stuff 'second hand'. She was probably its third or fourth owner, each piece displaying a series of dents and scratches from each of its previous lives.

But so what?

If he looked hard enough, Alex would notice what was really important. And that was that she kept the place immaculately clean and tidy.

She tossed her head, angled her chin into the air and said coolly, 'Yes, this is where I live. Sorry if it's not up to your high standards, but we can't all be as rich as you. What are you doing here, Alex? How did you find me?'

'I'm here because you ran out on me before we finished our conversation,' he said through clenched teeth. 'As to finding you, that was easy. You were seen getting into a Lime Taxi. Discovering where it had dropped you didn't take long.'

'That's an invasion of privacy. They had no right to tell you where I'd gone.'

'Tell that to someone who cares.' Alex slammed the door behind him and moved determinedly towards her.

Katrina, who had managed to stand her ground at the bank earlier in the day, backed away from him.

His eyes were a glittering, angry blue, his jaw squared with the same emotion. He also looked impossibly, wickedly handsome, and the closer he moved into her personal space the more she was aware of him.

Her heart and her pulse rate both picked up rhythm.

Her back came up against the wall that divided the small living area from the even tinier kitchen. She pressed against it, as if she could somehow go through the painted brick to the other side.

Alex planted a hand against the wall on either side of her head, effectively trapping her.

His heat and his smell were all around her.

Anxiety and awareness coursed through her, making her tremble.

'That's the second time you've run out on me. And the last. Understand?' Alex said in a dangerously soft voice, his breath wafting across her face.

'I didn't run out on you,' she said, angling her chin into the air. 'I walked.'

He growled something completely incomprehensible under his breath. 'Don't split hairs. Why did you leave?'

She snatched in a breath. 'I left because I didn't like what you were saying.'

'So why didn't you just tell me that?'

'I did. I said I wasn't going to sign your stupid document. And I'm not,' she added for good measure. 'I haven't changed my mind.'

He bared his teeth in the parody of a smile. 'You will if you know what's good for you.'

The threat stirred her anger to life. She welcomed the emotion because it banished her awareness of him.

'No, I won't.' She dug the point of her index finger into the centre of his chest. 'Because Sam *is* your daughter.'

He froze, face twisting. 'Stop saying that. It's not true!'

Her anger evaporated as if it had never existed. Her heart stilled then took off at a gallop. A shiver made its way down and then up her spine, setting her teeth on edge.

For the first time, she appreciated just how much Alex didn't want it to be true.

She frowned. Surely this was more than just the normal reaction of a playboy who didn't want to be tied down? She could practically feel the anxiety seeping out of his pores into the air surrounding them.

Something else was going on here, although she didn't have a clue what it was.

'Yes, Alex. It is.'

'It's not. It can't be.' Alex couldn't hide the desperation in his voice. It was clear he was in some form of denial, which meant he was in for a rude awakening.

'I'm afraid it is.' She paused for a moment before playing the ace she'd hoped wouldn't be required. 'And I can prove it.'

He raised a dark eyebrow. 'And just how do you plan on doing that?'

'A DNA test will prove Sam's paternity.'

Alex was such a logical, facts-and-figures kind of guy. He would have no choice but to believe scientific evidence.

The suggestion had clearly shocked Alex. He was staring at her as if she'd just grown three heads.

While she waited for him to say something, Katrina couldn't stop her eyes from running over him.

There wasn't a man alive who looked as good in a suit as Alex did. All of his clothes were handmade and fitted him like a glove. He was tall and lean, with broad shoulders, a muscled chest and long, powerful legs. The dark fabric accentuated his black hair and piercing blue eyes.

He looked elegant and sophisticated and very, very male.

Heat stirred low in her pelvis. She was nowhere near as immune to him as she liked to think she was. He'd been right when he said her eyes had eaten him up as soon as she'd burst into the boardroom. They were eating him up again now. She couldn't seem to help herself.

And she didn't understand why.

The way he'd treated her should have killed all of the feelings she had for him. And it had—at least on an emotional level. She hadn't been lying when she'd told Alex she didn't love him any more.

Because she didn't. If anything, the reverse was true.

But, on a physical level, it was a different matter entirely.

Physically, she was as attracted to him as the day they'd first met.

She'd pushed open the boardroom door, taken one look at Alex and now the burn was back.

Just like that.

'Are you serious about this?' Alex asked, interrupting her thoughts.

Katrina dragged her eyes back to his face, hoping he hadn't noticed the way she'd been staring at him. 'Frankly, I'd rather not have to go through the humiliation of everyone knowing that you think I sleep around. But if it's the only way you'll accept the truth then I'm more than willing to go through with it.'

'In that case, I'll arrange the test.' His expression gave nothing away. If he had doubts, he wasn't showing them. He glanced at his watch. 'There's no time like the present. The sooner we get this farce over with, the better.'

Alex didn't say a word as the doctor swabbed the inside of the baby's cheek then put the spatula in a thin glass testtube and marked the outside with a bar-coded sticker.

'How soon can we have the results?' he demanded as Dr Kershew extracted a fresh applicator.

'It will take forty-eight hours,' Doctor Kershew replied. 'Open up.'

Alex opened his mouth. The doctor repeated the process on the inside of his mouth.

'Can't you get it done any faster?' Alex asked with a frown as soon as the doctor was finished.

Doctor Kershew placed the two samples side by side on his cluttered desk then looked back and forth between them. He was obviously aware of the tension that had been simmering between them since they'd entered the surgery ten minutes ago. 'I'll see what I can do.'

'You'll call me as soon as you know?' Alex pressed.

Doctor Kershew shook his head. 'They don't call

with the results. They send a written report. Would you like it sent to your home or office?'

'My home. The less people who know about this, the better,' he stated grimly, with a sharp glance in Katrina's direction.

Katrina's response was to jut her chin into the air, and her cat-like green eyes glinted with challenge again.

'And you, Ms Ashby? Where would you like your copy sent?'

She turned to the doctor. 'I don't need it.' She flung Alex a look that he was sure could strip paint. 'I already know what the results will be. I don't need some silly test to tell me something I already know.'

Alex stared at her, his scalp contracting. He'd been discomfited when she'd suggested the DNA testing. Hell, he'd been more than uncomfortable. He'd felt as though she'd smacked him around the head with a plank of wood.

If she'd had any doubts about the child's parentage, then surely she'd have avoided the suggestion like the plague?

Now she was acting supremely confident of the results, so much so that the back of his neck began to prickle and a restless sensation attacked the base of his spine.

What if she was right?

What if the child was his?

Alex let his eyes stray to the baby's cot, which so far he'd avoided looking at.

The baby had fallen into a peaceful sleep, her tiny fist pressed against her flushed cheek, her bow-like mouth softly parted, her little chest rising and falling with each breath.

He'd decided many years ago never to get married

or have children. With his family history, he'd considered it his only option.

It was a decision he'd never regretted.

He'd never even thought about what it would be like to have a child. What was the point when he'd already decided not to?

Now he had to consider it.

He stared at the sleeping infant. She was cute, he had to admit that. But then so was a newborn kitten. But if she was his...

The breath caught in the back of his throat.

If she was his then it was a different matter entirely.

Alex sucked in a deep breath and dragged his gaze away from the cot. His eyes locked with Katrina's. She'd noticed him watching the child. She had a very assessing look on her face, as if she was trying to figure out what he was thinking.

She'd be surprised if she could look inside his head, Alex acknowledged wryly, because his thoughts had just jumped to another aspect of their situation.

If the child was his, then it meant Katrina hadn't betrayed him.

There had been no other man.

No other lover.

And no intention to scam him.

It also meant that what they'd shared was real.

He wasn't quite sure why that was so important to him but it was.

'It's standard procedure,' the doctor said gently. 'Both parents receive a copy.'

Katrina looked back at the doctor and shrugged. 'I don't care where you send it.'

'Oh, for goodness' sake!' Alex rattled off the address.

The doctor made a note on the file before shutting it closed. 'There, all done. Now, if that's all, I'd better see to my next patient. I'm behind schedule.'

'Thank you for squeezing us in,' Alex said, rising to his feet. 'I appreciate it.'

'You said it was important. I always have time for you and your family.' He leaned confidingly towards Katrina. 'I delivered Alex and his brother, you know. I have a soft spot for them.'

'I can imagine,' she said faintly.

The doctor looked back at Alex. 'How is Michael doing?'

Tension gripped him. 'The same,' he bit out. He didn't want to talk about his brother in front of Katrina.

The doctor shook his head sadly. 'Well, if there's anything I can do, all you have to do is call.'

'I know. But the first step is up to Michael.'

Katrina was paying close attention to the conversation. Alex had made a point of keeping his family and Katrina apart, as he did with all of his lovers. He'd wanted to avoid building any expectation of a permanent relationship.

But more and more that looked like it had been a waste of time where Katrina was concerned.

Because, if the baby did turn out to be his, then the future he'd envisaged would be well and truly blown to smithereens.

Alex was trying and failing to process an inbox full of emails when Royce called at eight that night. Once again, the other man got straight to the point. 'I don't have a lot to report. One of my people has been watching the apartment since just before you arrived at two-oh-three.'

Alex was impressed they'd moved so quickly. 'And…?'

'And nothing. Katrina came out with a pram around three-thirty and walked to the local park and back. Other than that she hasn't been out. A number of people have come and gone from the apartment building, but it's been difficult to ascertain whether any of them have visited her. There's been no sign of the guy who owns the apartment.'

Alex stiffened. 'What guy?'

'Let me see.' Alex heard the tapping of computer keys. 'The apartment is owned by a guy called Peter Strauss.'

Something shifted in his chest. 'She's living with a man?'

'That's not clear. We're still looking into it. Katrina's name doesn't appear on any official lease or documentation. At least none that we've found so far. She's either living with the guy or she has a private arrangement with him.'

'I see,' Alex said, not seeing at all, and wishing to hell that he did. 'What else do you know about the guy?'

'Nothing. We're doing a background check now. I should have an answer for you tomorrow or the day after.'

'Make it tomorrow. I want to know everything. When they met. What their relationship is. Everything.'

Alex wasn't sure why he was so interested.

He tried to tell himself it was because the Strauss chap could be the baby's father, but he knew he was just fooling himself.

He was a great believer in the saying 'actions speak

louder than words' and Katrina's behaviour suggested she was telling the truth.

The scales were now firmly tipped in favour of him being the child's father.

So why should he care who this guy was?

Frankly he shouldn't give a flying fig, but he did.

Alex sat stiffly in his chair, body so tense he expected his joints to creak when he moved. A restless sensation attacked the bottom of his spine.

He wanted to storm over to the apartment and demand some answers.

Instead, he cursed under his breath and headed for his bedroom. He pulled on a pair of black running shorts, a white singlet top and a pair of trainers. Leaving the apartment by his private elevator, he headed for the nearby park.

He jogged for an hour most days.

Tonight, he didn't jog.

Tonight, he pounded the pavement as if his very life depended on it.

Sweat dripped from his body.

His lungs burned and his heart raced.

On his twelfth lap, Alex decided to call it quits. He could run until he cut a groove in the cement and it still wouldn't ease his frustration.

He ground to a sudden halt, gasped in a breath and swore viciously.

Jogging at a less frantic pace, he headed back to his apartment.

Then, sweaty, tired and so wired he expected to emit sparks at any moment, he snatched up his car keys.

CHAPTER THREE

KATRINA was cleaning the kitchen sink—gleaming stainless-steel was almost as satisfying as glowing white ceramic—when someone pounded on the door as if they were trying to smash it down.

Worried the racket might wake Samantha, she removed her rubber gloves and hurried to the door.

'Who is it?' she called softly, trying to keep her voice down.

'It's Alex. Open up!'

'Alex?' she asked in surprise, blonde eyebrows shooting towards her hairline.

What was Alex doing here?

'Yes. Alex. Open the door!'

Startled by his forceful order, Katrina slid the door chain along its protective channel and then turned her attention to the lock. In her nervous haste, and hindered by the oversized rubber gloves, her fingers fumbled with the latch and it took her two attempts to get the door open.

'What do you want, Alex?' she asked.

Although she hadn't invited him in, Alex swept past her into the apartment.

As he did, she noticed what he was wearing.

Or, rather, what he *wasn't* wearing.

All he had on was running gear. Skimpy running-gear that left very little to the imagination.

A white singlet top bared the steely strength of his broad, bronzed shoulders, and short shorts left the hair-roughened length of his powerful legs free for her hungry gaze to feast upon.

In an instant, her mouth was parchment dry and her heart was beating ninety-to-the-dozen. 'Alex?' she prompted when he failed to answer her.

Suddenly she realised that while she'd been staring at Alex he'd been staring just as hard at her.

In her eagerness to open the door before Samantha was disturbed, Katrina had forgotten she was wearing her oldest tracksuit. It was tatty and worn, and the black was no longer sharp but faded. She'd taken the jacket off a while ago; scrubbing was hot work. Beneath it she was wearing a black stretchy top with spaghetti-thin straps.

If her outfit wasn't bad enough, her hair had fallen out of the clip she'd used to fasten it to the top of her head. It was now half up and half down, with several strands sticking to her cheeks. To top everything else off, she wasn't wearing a touch of make-up—not even mascara.

Katrina cringed inside at her dowdy appearance and then immediately reprimanded herself.

Who cared what Alex thought?

It wasn't as though he meant anything to her any more.

'What are you doing here, Alex?'

Alex stared at her with hooded eyes, then said abruptly, 'I thought you lived alone.'

Katrina blinked at the comment, which had come out of left field. 'I do. Apart from Sam, of course,' she said, trying to ignore how primal and potently make Alex looked.

'Really?' He raised a brow. 'What about Peter Strauss?'

Katrina blinked again. How did he know about Peter? And why was he asked about him?

'Peter is my landlord,' she said automatically.

'You don't have a lease.'

It was a statement not a question, and it was fired at her as fast as a bullet from a gun.

An uneasy feeling settled at the base of her spine. 'How do you know that?'

He waved a hand. 'Just answer the question.'

'Have you had me investigated?' she asked, still preoccupied with how he'd come across the information.

'Of course.'

Shock ratcheted up her spine, vertebra by vertebra. 'How dare you?'

'Oh, I dare a lot of things. Why should you care, anyway?' His eyes narrowed. 'Unless you've got something to hide?'

'I've got nothing to hide.'

'Then why won't you answer the question?'

Katrina folded her arms. 'Because it's none of your business, that's why! As far as I'm concerned, you have no right to question me—unless it relates to Sam.'

His eyes flashed with an emotion she couldn't quite define. Suddenly, he was right there in front of her, hand cupping her throat. 'Answer the question!'

The smell of heated male flesh mixed with sweat folded around her like an invisible cloak. As she inhaled, it was as if she were absorbing little particles of Alex that circulated in her bloodstream like a potent drug.

Swallowing against the warmth of his palm, she managed to say huskily, 'What's this all about, Alex?'

What's this all about?

That was a good question, Alex decided.

It was just a shame he didn't have an answer.

At least not one he wanted to share.

He didn't want to admit—even to himself—that jealousy had sent him rushing over here like a man possessed. But there was no other explanation.

And the little green monster was having a field day, eating away at him like acid burning through metal.

Katrina looked unbelievably sexy in an entirely natural way. She might not be wearing any make-up, and her outfit was one that most of his previous lovers would have consigned to the rubbish bin, but all Alex could see was the shapely contours of her body, skin that was glowing with good health and hair that was shining with vitality.

Had Strauss seen Katrina dressed like this? Had he peeled the figure-hugging black top and faded tracksuit-bottoms off the sleek lines of her body before making love to her?

'Who is Peter Strauss to you?' He knew he shouldn't ask the question but was unable to hold it back.

She stiffened beneath the loose hold he had on her throat and her cat-like green eyes flashed quick-silver. '*That* is none of your business. Our relationship is over, remember?' she said, tossing her head.

Her fragrance filtered into the air. Alex inhaled without meaning to, filling his lungs with the smell of her.

His head spun.

His heart pounded.

His body hardened.

Let her go, a little voice in his head instructed with warning. *Let her go before you do something stupid.*

Alex prided himself on his logic. The little voice in his head made a lot of sense.

Still, Alex couldn't bring himself to release her.

Frustration imploded inside of him.

She was right.

He knew she was right.

'I don't care who you sleep with,' Alex said harshly, wondering whether she knew he was lying through his teeth. 'You can sleep with ten men for all I care.' If she did, he would commit murder. 'I'm thinking of the child. She needs to be brought up in a moral environment.'

'The *child* has a name,' Katrina said pointedly. 'And I think that's a little bit rich coming from you!'

'Meaning?'

'Meaning you've had more women than you can probably count, so I don't think you should be pointing fingers.'

His fingers curled more closely around her throat. 'Don't push me, Katrina.'

'Or what? What will you do? Kiss me again like you did this morning?' she goaded.

His eyes dropped to her mouth. She had the most beautiful mouth, just made for kissing.

'Yes,' he said huskily, and did what he'd wanted to do since he'd walked into the room.

Acting on gut instinct, he bent his head and claimed her mouth with his.

Unlike this morning, Katrina didn't put up even a show of resistance.

This time, she kissed him right back with a depth of hunger that struck deep inside him.

Groaning in the back of his throat, Alex hooked an arm around the small of her back and pulled her closer until nothing, not even air, came between them.

He ignored the fact that their relationship was over and he shouldn't be kissing her at all.

He ignored the fact that a young child, in all likelihood his daughter, lay sleeping innocently in the bedroom behind them.

He ignored everything except touching her and tasting her and relishing the familiar feel of her in his arms.

He deepened the kiss. Her arms made their way up and around his neck, where she dug her fingers into his hair.

The flash-fire of primitive desire laid claim to every ounce of tissue in his body. Muscles strained to get closer to her. His skin shrank around his bones. His heart and his pulse didn't feel as if they belonged to him as they beat out a frantic tattoo.

He urged her backwards, instinctively seeking and finding the lounge. The backs of her knees hit the edge of a seat and he tumbled her on to the cushions.

He looked down. One spaghetti-thin strap had slipped off a creamy shoulder, baring the swell of her breast to his gaze.

His body throbbed—hard.

And, then again, even harder.

Then his eyes landed on a stuffed toy sitting in the corner of the lounge.

It was a brown gorilla. And it appeared to be staring at him.

Alex froze.

This was madness. Absolute and utter madness.

Until this situation was sorted, he shouldn't be touching her.

He took a step backwards.

And then another.

Then he said, 'We can't do this.'

Katrina flopped back against the sofa.

She was weak, breathing heavily, body pulsing.

He was right; they shouldn't be doing this.

She closed her eyes.

Why, oh why, had she let Alex kiss her? And why, oh why, had she kissed him back? He thought she was a liar and a cheat. He thought she was low enough to try and foist another man's child on him. She needed her head read for letting him anywhere near her.

She breathed in deeply and willed her heart to stop its frantic beating.

'I think you'd better leave,' she murmured without looking at him.

Katrina could feel him looking at her bent head.

'Are you OK?' he asked finally.

Her eyes snapped open before flashing to his. 'I'm fine. Why wouldn't I be?'

'Why indeed?'

Alex walked to the door and pulled it open. 'I'll call you when I get the results.'

'You do that,' she said, just before the door closed with a quiet click.

* * *

Katrina was cleaning the fridge two days later, trying to take her mind off the fact that today was the day the DNA test results were due, when the doorbell rang.

Immediately, she tensed.

What if it was Alex?

She hadn't received her set of results yet, but that didn't mean Alex hadn't received his.

How was he going to react to the news that Samantha was indeed his daughter?

Stripping off her green rubber-gloves, she tossed them on to the sideboard before hurrying to the door. She paused and took a deep breath before pulling it open.

It was Alex.

But it was an Alex she'd never seen before.

He looked ill. Grey. Strained. Older.

She gripped his arm, which was rock-hard with tension.

'Alex, what's wrong? Are you sick? Do you want me to call a doctor?'

He shook his head but didn't answer her.

She all but pulled him into the apartment.

It was then she noticed the piece of paper gripped in his clenched fist.

Her heart plummeted to her toes with sickening speed, then jolted into the back of her throat.

'Is that…is that the test results?' she choked out.

Alex looked at his hand as if surprised to see he was still clutching the document.

He nodded, his fist unclenching as if it was spring loaded.

The paper bearing the logo of the laboratory dropped to the carpet.

Katrina didn't bother picking it up. Didn't bother because she knew the results.

Alex lifted his head and stared at her. His face was empty of expression and Katrina registered that he was in some kind of shock.

'Samantha is my daughter,' he said simply, his voice so low she could barely hear him.

Katrina nodded.

'I'm a father,' he croaked.

Again, she nodded. 'Yes. Yes, you are.'

He ran a hand through his hair and around the back of his neck. 'I thought I was prepared for this. When you suggested the DNA test, I knew you had to be pretty sure I was the father. But seeing it in black and white...' He shook his head. 'It's knocked me for six.'

Katrina could see that. She'd never seen Alex like this.

But she found it hard to be sympathetic. She'd told him the truth so many times, she'd practically turned blue in the face. But he hadn't listened to her.

Not once.

Even when she'd suggested the DNA test he hadn't given her an inch.

'Do you have something to drink?' Alex asked.

'I presume you're not referring to tea or coffee?'

'Whiskey, if you have it?'

'I think Peter has some,' she said.

She went to the kitchen cabinet where Peter kept his alcohol. Finding a bottle of whiskey towards the back, she poured a decent measure into a tumbler she pulled from the adjoining cupboard.

'Here,' she said, holding the glass out towards him.

Alex walked towards her as stiffly as a store mannequin come to life, took the glass and threw the whiskey down his throat in one fell swoop. The liquid must have burned on the way down, but he looked like he relished the sensation, and when he turned towards her a moment later the spark of life was back in his eyes.

'I want to see her.' His voice was stronger now, his face determined. This was the Alex she knew so well. The successful businessman who knew exactly where he was going and what he wanted.

'Of course.' Katrina didn't hesitate. She'd approached Alex because she wanted him to be a part of Samantha's life. It looked like that started now. She pointed to the corner of the room near the window. 'She's in her pram.'

He nodded. His eyes were fixed with unwavering concentration on the pram as he crossed the room and looked down.

Alex bent over the pram, his heart kicking like a bucking bronco in his chest.

As soon as he did so, the baby smiled up at him.

She had his eyes, Alex realised, his heart squeezing tight in his chest, an emotion he hadn't felt before blossoming inside him.

Or had she?

Didn't all babies have blue eyes when they were born?

He wasn't sure, but he preferred to think she took after him.

'Hello, Samantha,' he said, his voice little more than a croak, his throat so tight he could barely speak.

The baby gurgled and thrashed her little arms and legs.

She was wearing some pink all-in-one thing with a

bright-pink bunny motif on her chest. She looked so cute, his heart wrenched again.

'She's beautiful.'

Katrina appeared in his peripheral vision. 'Yes. Yes, she is.'

'She's so tiny.'

Katrina laughed. 'She may be small, but she has a good set of lungs on her.'

He turned, a smile tilting the corners of his mouth. 'Does she?'

Katrina nodded. 'Yes. She's a determined little miss. I'd say she takes after you in that regard. When she's hungry, or needs changing, she makes sure everyone in a ten-mile radius know about it.'

'How old is she?' he asked, staring back into the pram.

'She was born on the nineteenth of April, so she's a little over seven weeks old. She weighed two-point-eight kilograms and was fifty-point-seven centimetres long.'

Alex felt his heart turn over. 'I wish I'd been there to see her born.' For the first time, he thought about what Katrina must have gone through. 'Was it a difficult birth?'

She shrugged. 'Difficult enough, I suppose. I was in labour for twenty-one hours.'

'But you're all right?'

She nodded. 'I'm fine.'

'And Samantha?'

'She's fine too.' She smiled. 'She has all her fingers and toes.'

'I should have been there,' he ground out, hands clenched into fists at his side.

Guilt ate into him.

He'd spent years trying not to follow in his father's footsteps.

And on a business front he'd succeeded.

More than succeeded.

He'd worked two jobs to pay for his university fees. He'd studied when other students had been out partying. And when he'd got his first real job he'd worked his tail off, clawing his way to the top with sheer grit and determination.

On a personal front, it was a different story.

Although he was popular with the ladies, Alex didn't want to have the kind of relationship his parents had had. Marriage had trapped them in a cauldron of constant fighting and unhappiness.

He preferred to keep his relationships short, sweet and simple.

The minute things started to go south, he just walked away.

And as to having children? Well, they'd been off the agenda too.

Since his father's blood pumped through his veins, there was a chance—even if it was only a slim one— that he would follow in his father's footsteps.

After all, he'd inherited lots of other things from him: the physical resemblance was almost uncanny. Alex had seen photos of his father when he was younger, and it was like looking at a photo of himself as he was today.

But it was the other traits—little things that didn't mean a lot on their own but when put together meant something else entirely—that sent a chill down his spine.

They were both left-handed.

They were both allergic to peanuts and strawberries.

They both had a habit of running their hands through their hair and around the back of their necks. Every now and then, Alex would catch himself doing it and would shiver at the likeness.

The list was endless.

If he'd inherited all of those things, what was to say his father's abusive nature hadn't been inbred in him and was just waiting for the right time to show itself?

James Webber had abused his children without a second thought.

Alex had considered it far better not to have children in the first place than to risk hurting them later on.

But against all the odds he *had* become a father.

And what had he done?

The first thing he'd done was let his daughter down.

He'd abandoned Samantha—and Katrina—when they'd needed him.

Katrina moved away from him. 'Yes. You should have been.'

Alex stiffened at the recrimination in her voice. Although he had a lot to answer for, he was not alone in that. Anger crackled up his spine. 'I'm willing to take partial responsibility for what happened,' he said harshly. 'But so should you. If you hadn't disappeared the way you did, then we wouldn't be in this situation.'

She jutted her chin defiantly into the air, her eyes spitting emerald fire at him. 'Don't try to blame this on me, Alex. I told you I was pregnant with your child and all you did was insult me. You preferred to think I'd been sleeping around.'

'I told you I was in shock. You should have tried again.'

'Uh-uh. No way!' She shook her head vigorously

from side to side. 'Do you have any idea how offensive you were? Even if I'd been feeling one-hundred percent, I still wouldn't have wanted to face that again. And, since my morning sickness had well and truly kicked in by then the thought of confronting you made me want to throw up.'

Even though Alex had actively avoided having anything to do with children, and the families having them, he had heard enough to know how debilitating morning sickness could be. The fact that Katrina had suffered from it without his support merely deepened his guilt.

'OK. You've made your point. But do you realise it was less than forty-eight hours before I went to your apartment to talk to you?'

Her eyes spat that emerald fire at him again, until Alex half-expected his hair to catch fire. 'If you expect me to applaud you for that, then you're wrong. You should have followed me home straight away and apologised.'

Alex ran a hand through his hair and around the back of his neck, noticed what he was doing and ruthlessly dragged his hand back down to his side. 'You're right. I should have.'

'But you didn't. As a result, I went through my pregnancy and the birth alone without anyone there to support me.'

Alex clamped his hands into fists at his side, an invisible hand clawing at his insides. 'You had no one with you?'

'No.'

Alex turned back to the pram, not so much to look at his daughter as not to look at Katrina. He should have been there to provide her with the support she needed.

It was all well and good kicking himself now, but it couldn't undo the damage he'd done.

As if deciding that she preferred him smiling to scowling, Samantha suddenly started to cry. Despite the gravity of their conversation, Alex found himself smiling as the sound ripped into his eardrums. 'I see what you mean. That's some sound.'

'She's only just started. Give her a few minutes to get to full throttle, and you'll know what she's really capable of.'

Alex grimaced. 'God forbid!' He turned expectantly to Katrina. 'Aren't you supposed to pick her up when she cries?'

She gestured with one hand. 'You're the closest.'

Alex took a step back from the pram. And then another. His heart knocked on his breast bone. 'I couldn't. I might drop her.'

'I'm sure you won't. Just make sure you support her head and neck.'

Alex looked back into the pram. Samantha's face was rapidly changing from pale red to beetroot, and the volume of her cries had grown several decibels.

Dragging in a breath, he gingerly reached in and picked her up.

She weighed practically nothing and almost fit into the palms of his hands. 'You're just perfect, aren't you?' he whispered, feeling the truth of that statement reverberate deep inside him.

Samantha stopped crying and stared up at him. Carefully, he shifted her into the crook of his arm.

She smelled sweet—powdery. Babyish. Completely and utterly unique.

An invisible hand reached into his chest and clamped around his heart. He could hardly breathe, as if a steel band had been slipped around him and tightened until it hurt.

Samantha was his.

Flesh of his flesh.

Blood of his blood.

Something primitive surged inside.

He wanted to hug Samantha to his chest and never let go.

It was a deep-rooted feeling of possession he'd never felt before.

He looked at his daughter and felt tears sting the back of his eyes.

He stroked a gentle hand over her hair, several shades lighter than his own. 'My hair was that colour when I was born. It got darker as I got older.'

'No doubt Sam's will do the same,' Katrina acknowledged.

He swallowed, once. Twice. Three times.

He dragged in a breath. Then another.

And made a silent promise to his daughter—a promise to do all the things his father should have done but hadn't.

And a promise not to do the things his father should not have done but had.

Carefully, he held the baby out to Katrina. 'Here. You'd better take her.' He sniffed. 'I think she needs changing.'

Katrina took Samantha from him and walked to the small dining table, one end of which had been set up as a baby-change table.

Alex thrust his now-empty hands deep into his

trouser pockets as he watched Katrina expertly unsnap the fastenings of the jump suit and begin changing his daughter's nappy.

He'd wondered how he would feel if it turned out Samantha was his.

He now had his answer.

He felt lucky, privileged and terrified all at the same time.

CHAPTER FOUR

KATRINA put Samantha back in the pram and looked up. She found Alex staring at their daughter with an odd expression. 'What?'

He shook his head. 'I still can't believe she's mine.'

'I don't know why you're so surprised. As I told you before, one time using no protection is all it takes.'

'I know.' He gazed back steadily with eyes almost the exact same shade as his daughter's. 'But what you don't realise is that I had a vasectomy in my early twenties.'

Her mouth dropped open.

She blinked.

'What the—?' She snapped her mouth closed, dragged in a breath, and then another. 'You have to be joking?'

He shook his head. 'No. I'm perfectly serious.'

'But the condoms…?' She rubbed her temple, hoping the action would clear the fuzziness in her head— because she was very confused. 'Why would you insist on using condoms if you'd already had a vasectomy?'

'Condoms protect against disease as well as pregnancy, so I've made a habit of wearing them. Since you weren't on the Pill it made sense to keep on using them. If I hadn't, you'd have wondered why. And, frankly, I didn't want to discuss a personal decision which is nobody's business but my own.'

Katrina had heard every single word he'd said, but on one level they just didn't make sense. It was as if he had suddenly started speaking in another language.

'But why on earth would you have a vasectomy?' Katrina said, asking the very question he'd originally set out to avoid answering.

'I would have thought the reason was obvious.' He looked her straight in the eye and made no attempt to soften the blow he was about to deliver. 'Because I didn't want children.'

His answer sucked the air from her lungs. Her chest felt so tight she could hardly breathe. Her heart stopped, stammered and restarted with a wallop.

While she was still reeling, Alex continued. 'The doctor who performed the surgery explained that there was a certain failure rate with the procedure, but I had all the necessary tests and believed it was a success. Since Samantha is my daughter, then obviously it failed somehow.'

Katrina didn't comment. The whys and wherefores were of no interest to her. It was the bottom line that concerned her.

And the bottom line was that Alex didn't want children.

What did that mean for their little girl? she wondered, anxiety tearing her insides to shreds.

'Aren't you going to say "I told you so"?' Alex asked, raising an eyebrow.

She shrugged. 'What's the point? This isn't about who's right and who's wrong. This is about Sam. I only want what's best for her. That's all I've ever wanted.'

Alex grimaced. 'I'm sorry for doubting you.'

She barked out a harsh laugh that had no amusement in it. 'Considering what you've just told me, I suppose you had your reasons. But you still had no right to turn on me the way you did. You said some pretty horrible things to me. I never cheated on you, and I don't believe I ever behaved in a way to suggest that I would. The least you could have done was give me the benefit of the doubt.'

'You're right. I'm sorry.'

Katrina inclined her head. 'Apology accepted.'

He looked surprised but pleased by her response. 'Good. Then we can move forward with a clean slate.'

'And what exactly does moving forward mean? If you don't want children, does that mean you don't want Sam? Because I'll tell you here and now that I want her to have both of her parents in her life. It's important to me.' To emphasise just how important, she added, 'Sam has no other blood relatives on my side of the family. If something happens to me, she's going to need you. I don't want her to be put into an orphanage or the foster-care system. She deserves more than that.'

'You're young and healthy. There's no reason to expect anything will happen to you for many years to come.'

'I'm not willing to take the chance. Accidents happen all the time. And the risk of me not being in her life when she's older is higher than I'd like.' At his enquiring look, she added huskily, 'Breast cancer runs in my family. I lost my grandmother, my aunt and my mother to the disease. I don't like my odds of not getting it.'

His frown deepened. 'Aren't there tests for that kind of thing?'

She nodded. 'Yes, although all it can do is identify whether I have the gene or not, not if I'll get the disease.'

'And you've had the test?'

She nodded.

'And…?'

'And I have the gene,' she replied simply.

Alex paled beneath his skin. 'And there's nothing they can do?'

'I could have a double mastectomy, but I'm not ready to do that. I want more children, and I'd rather breast feed them if I can.' She shrugged. 'Regular mammograms and self-examination is about all I can do—apart from taking care of my overall health, of course.'

Alex just stared at her. It was clear he was stunned by what she'd told him.

'But can you see why it's so important to me that she has both of us?' Katrina said softly.

He nodded. 'Well, you can set your mind at ease. I have every intention of being a part of Samantha's life.'

Relief swept through her, unknotting muscles she hadn't even known she'd had. 'That's great.'

Alex stared at her, face expressionless. She couldn't tell what he was thinking but for some reason she began to feel uneasy, a restless sensation attacking the base of her spine.

'So we're in agreement, then?' he asked. 'We have to do what's best for Samantha?'

Although the question appeared straightforward, there was an odd note in Alex's voice that she couldn't quite decipher. It made her unease expand quickly into out-and-out wariness. 'Of course. That's why I came back.'

But was it the only reason? a little voice whispered in her head.

A couple of days ago her answer would have been a clear and resounding yes.

But now Katrina wasn't so sure.

The way she'd kissed Alex two nights ago had thrown her thought processes into chaos.

She had a sneaky suspicion that a part of her had wanted to come back because she'd wanted to see Alex again.

'Good,' Alex said, breaking into her thoughts. 'Then the only logical course of action is for the two of you to move in with me.'

Katrina blinked. Dragged in a breath. Blinked again.

Surely she hadn't heard him right?

Because she thought he'd just said…

Well, she thought he'd just said…

She shook her head.

No. Whatever she thought she'd heard was wrong. It had to be.

'Say that again,' she said.

He didn't hesitate. 'You heard me. I want you and Samantha to move in with me as soon as it can possibly be arranged.'

The strength and conviction in his voice convinced her.

She'd heard him right the first time. And the second.

Katrina looked away from him.

His suggestion had caught her way off-guard. Whatever she'd expected him to say, it wasn't that.

Bitter irony pinched at her insides with razor-sharp claws. There was a time when she'd wanted nothing more than to live with Alex. If he'd asked her a year ago she'd have been over the moon.

But he hadn't asked, so there was no point wishing he had.

And now…

Well, as far as she was concerned, it was much too late.

'I thought you didn't do permanent live-in relationships?' she said, referring to the warning he'd given her when they'd first started sleeping together.

'I don't. Or, at least, I didn't. But circumstances have changed somewhat, wouldn't you say?' he said, with a pointed glance at the pram.

Katrina followed his gaze. 'I suppose they have.' She looked back at him. 'So you're prepared to sacrifice your freedom for Sam—is that what you're saying?'

'I wouldn't put it exactly like that but, essentially, yes.'

His answer shouldn't have hurt but it did.

Those pincers went to work on her insides again, this time getting their razor-sharp edges into the centre of her heart.

Katrina didn't understand her reaction. She didn't love Alex any more. Why should she care that he was prepared to give up his freedom for his daughter when he hadn't cared enough for her to do the same?

'Well…?' Alex prompted when she just stared at him.

'I hardly think living together is necessary,' she said in a cool voice.

'Well, I do.'

She'd heard that tone before. It was the 'I always get what I want, so you might as well give in now' tone.

Well, he wasn't getting what he wanted this time.

Angling her chin, she said, 'Well, that's too bad. I don't want to live with you.'

Alex frowned, clearly surprised by her response. No doubt he'd expected her just to blindly do what she was told.

She could understand why he thought that; once upon a time, that was exactly what she would have done.

But not now.

Becoming a mother had changed her. She had more than just herself to think about now.

She could no longer avoid conversations or situations she wasn't comfortable with. Not when they affected Samantha. Her daughter had to come first.

'I insist.' His tone was smooth but underlined by steel.

'You can insist all you like, but it won't change my mind.' She splayed her hands out wide and adopted a conciliatory tone; arguing wasn't going to get them anywhere. 'If you're worried about access, then don't be. I won't fight you regarding visitation. You can see as much of Sam as you like. I don't want there to be a tug-of-war between us, nor do I ever want her to feel as if she has to choose between us.'

'She won't have to. Because we'll be living together.'

The phrase 'immovable object' immediately sprang into her mind.

Alex could be both stubborn and determined. Those qualities had certainly helped him to become the success he was today. But they could also be extremely annoying.

Because if he thought she was going to move in with him after the way he'd treated her, then he was out of his mind.

'It's the only practical solution. I want to see Samantha every day, not when some schedule tells me I can.' Alex held up a hand as she opened her mouth to speak. 'And don't tell me there wouldn't be some kind of timetable, because we both know there would have to be.'

She sighed. 'OK. I suppose you have a point. But you need to look at the big picture.'

He raised an eyebrow. 'I thought that was exactly what I was doing. Isn't raising Samantha in a family environment the best thing for her?'

'In a real family the mother and father usually love each other,' Katrina shot back. 'That hardly applies in our case.'

'Love is a highly overrated emotion. It doesn't pay the bills and it doesn't keep you warm at night.' Tension drew his shoulders up towards his ears. 'I've seen some pretty horrible things done in the name of love. Frankly, I don't want anything to do with it.'

'If that's the case, then I feel sorry for you. You're going to miss out on so much. But we're straying from the point. What effect do you think living with the two of us will have on Sam? We do nothing but argue. That's hardly a healthy atmosphere for a child to grow up in.'

He gave her a meaningful look. 'I think what happened in this very room two nights ago proves we do more than argue.'

Colour swept up her neck and into her face. 'Hang on a minute. Let me get this straight—when you suggested we move in with you, I thought you were talking about a platonic arrangement. Kind of like one of those marriages of convenience but without the marriage. Are you now suggesting we live together for real? That you and I…?' She stopped and licked her lips. 'Resume intimate relations?'

'Intimate relations? If by that you mean having sex then, yes, that's exactly what I'm suggesting. The aim is to provide Samantha with a *real* family with all that that entails.'

Alex had briefly considered asking Katrina to marry him but had quickly dismissed it as an option.

The DNA test had provided his legal claim to his daughter and living together offered more flexibility. He also liked the idea of being able to walk away if things started to go wrong.

'Sex is hardly a sound basis to build a relationship on,' Katrina said scathingly.

'It's better than having nothing,' Alex shot back with the speed of light. He was determined to get what he wanted, and he was prepared to hammer each and every one of Katrina's arguments into the ground if that was what it was going to take. 'There have been plenty of relationships that have survived with far less. I always thought our physical relationship was rather special. I consider that a real bonus. Besides, aren't you ignoring the fact that we used to get on pretty well?'

'*Used to*, Alex. Past tense. I haven't noticed us getting along too well since I came back.' She shook her head. 'It would never work.'

'How do you know? How can either of us know?' He paused before saying softly, 'But don't you think we owe it to Samantha to try?'

Katrina bit down on her lower lip.

She was obviously thinking about it.

Their daughter was her weak point—a fact that he would use to his advantage.

He would do anything and everything within his power to make Katrina agree to move in with him.

After what seemed like for ever, Katrina slowly shook her head. 'I can't. To put it bluntly, I don't want to get involved with you again. After the way you've treated me, I don't think I can trust you again.'

Alex moved closer to her, his face determined. 'Just

fifteen minutes ago I apologised for those things and you accepted. We agreed we would move forward with a clean slate.'

Katrina frowned. 'You're right, I did. But that only extends so far.'

'A conditional acceptance?' Alex asked with a raised eyebrows.

She nodded. 'If you want to put it that way, then, yes. When I accepted your apology it meant that I'm willing to be civil to you whenever we meet. It also means I'm prepared to work together with you to decide what's best for Sam. It *doesn't* mean I either want to move in with you or start sleeping with you again.'

Alex wagged a finger at her. 'Ah, but now you're contradicting yourself.'

She frowned more deeply, clearly confused. 'And how am I doing that?'

'Aren't you the one who said this was about Samantha?'

She nodded. 'That's what I said. So…?'

'So you're making this all about you and what you want, not what's best for her.'

He heard her sharp inhalation of breath. Saw her eyes widen.

The room fell silent.

Alex waited for a moment and then went for the jugular. 'I'm willing to sacrifice my freedom to give Sam the family she deserves. What are you prepared to sacrifice?'

He'd used the shortened version of their daughter's name quite deliberately. He was playing on Katrina's emotions, but he didn't care.

He had to convince her that moving in with him was the right thing to do.

He intended to be a good father to Samantha, and he couldn't do that if she was living somewhere else.

Honesty also forced him to admit that this wasn't just about Samantha.

This was also about the fact that he wanted Katrina. What had happened here two nights ago proved that beyond a shadow of a doubt.

As he'd just told her, he'd always thought that what they'd shared was special.

So special, in fact, that he wasn't ready to let it go.

Finally, Katrina cleared her throat. 'You're suggesting I sacrifice myself for my daughter?'

'That's a rather melodramatic way of putting it but, yes, that's exactly what I'm suggesting. Besides we both know there wouldn't be any sacrifice involved,' Alex continued confidently. 'You want me.'

Katrina stared at him but didn't answer.

Alex smiled. 'I've kissed you twice in as many days and you've kissed me back both times.'

Her chin made its way into the air. Still, she didn't say anything.

His smile widened. 'Don't worry. You don't need to say anything. I know.'

She tossed her head, sending her caramel-coloured hair swirling around her shoulders. 'You're not omniscient, Alex. You don't know everything.'

His eyes dropped to her mouth. 'I know that it would only take one kiss to prove me right. Shall we try it?'

He crossed the room at the speed of light, grasped her hands and pulled her against him.

She tore herself out of his arms and took a stumbling step backwards. 'No.'

Alex followed her retreat and slid an arm around the small of her back. 'No? You don't sound very sure.'

Again, she wrenched herself out of his arms. This time she put the length of the sofa between them. 'I'm sure.'

Alex eyed the sofa separating them. If Katrina thought that would stop him if he really wanted to get to her, then she had another thing coming.

He shook his head, his mouth quirking at the corners. 'Really? I don't think you are.'

She blinked.

'Remember how you used to cry out my name when I sucked on your nipples?' She licked her lips as if they were dry; colour swept into her cheeks. 'And how you used to dig your nails into my back as you came? You drew blood on more than one occasion.'

The colour in her cheeks deepened until they were burning a bright pink. Her pupils dilated, the golden-brown flecks standing out prominently. Her chest was rising and falling, her nipples pressing against the tan cotton of her top.

'Remember?' he prompted again, his voice thickening.

She licked her lips again. 'I don't remember a thing.'

He crossed the room in a flash, practically vaulting the corner of the sofa. While she was still staring at him, open-mouthed, he pulled her into his arms and said huskily, 'Then let me remind you.'

Katrina shuddered as his mouth claimed hers.

No matter what she'd told Alex, she wanted him.

She might not love him any more, but the chemistry

between them was like an addiction that she had no control over.

Because, instead of pushing him away, she was winding her arms around his neck and pushing her aching breasts against the hard wall of his chest.

And, instead of telling him to get away from her, she was sighing her surrender into his mouth as if this was the first and last place she wanted to be.

Alex prised her lips apart and deepened the kiss. Their mouths danced a duel as erotic and as ageless as time. Light bloomed behind her closed eyelids. Heat blossomed under her skin until she felt as if she were glowing.

Alex lifted his head.

Her lashes fluttered open.

Their eyes met.

'Tell me,' he ordered, feeding a hand into her hair and pulling her head back to expose the fragile length of her neck.

Katrina let her eyes flutter closed again as she felt his mouth nip at the sensitive skin just below her ear. 'Yes,' she breathed.

'Yes what?' he asked, nipping at her again.

She opened her mouth to say the fateful words, 'yes, I want you', but at that exact moment Samantha began to cry.

My God, what was she doing? Katrina asked herself frantically.

She tore herself out of Alex's arms and stumbled towards the pram.

She dragged in a breath and released it slowly, then repeated the process. Gradually, her heartbeat began to slow towards the semblance of a normal rhythm.

When she was calm, she reached into the pram and picked Samantha up. 'Hush, little one. Hush.'

She gently rocked the baby until she quieted then looked at Alex. 'I am *not* going to sleep with you.'

Alex folded his arms across his impressive chest. 'Who are you trying to convince—me? Or yourself? You want me.'

It wasn't a question. It was a statement.

Katrina knew she would be wasting her breath trying to deny it. After the way she'd just kissed him, there was no doubt in either of their minds that he'd spoken the truth.

She tossed her head. 'So what if I do? Didn't your mother ever tell you that you can't always have what you want?'

His mouth twisted. 'Oh, she taught me that, all right.'

The bitterness in his voice immediately roused her curiosity, but satisfying it was hardly a priority.

Sorting out Samantha's future was the only thing that concerned her. And there was one thing she knew for sure.

She looked Alex squarely in the eye. 'I'm sorry, Alex, but I'm not prepared to live with you.'

Alex shook his head, his eyes showing a mixture of surprise and admiration. 'You really have changed, haven't you? You've turned into Little Miss Confrontation.'

She nodded. 'You'd better believe it. I used to be a pushover where you were concerned, but not any more. I can't forgive you for the way you treated me. At least, not enough to get involved with you again. It would make me unhappy, and that wouldn't be good for Sam.'

'And where does that leave me?' Alex challenged. 'Out in the cold?'

'Now who's the one being melodramatic?'

'I hardly think it's melodramatic when you're trying to stop me from being the father I want to be to Sam.' His eyes were as hard as nails, his voice threaded with the same steel. 'If that's your final decision, then you leave me no choice.'

The tone of his voice sent a chill unlike anything she'd known down her spine. A knot of tension formed in the base of her throat. 'What…what do you mean?'

'It means I intend to sue for sole custody.'

His answer sucked the air from her lungs.

'What—?' She stopped, swallowed and tried again. '*What* did you say?'

'You heard me.'

His voice was strong and determined; the look in his eyes was equally resolute.

Katrina staggered backwards.

Alex frowned and held out his hands. 'Give Sam to me before you drop her.'

Katrina backed out of reach, hugged her daughter close to her chest and wrapped her arms protectively around her. She glared at Alex. 'You stay away from her! And you can stay away from me too. In fact, I want you to leave. *Right now!*'

His hands dropped to his sides but he didn't move. A muscle along the line of his jaw bunched as if he were gritting his teeth. 'I'm not going anywhere.'

'I'll call the police,' she threatened.

'No, you won't.'

There it was again, that tone. Forceful. Attacking.

Like a compression wave travelling through the air. When it hit you, it threatened to strike you flat to the floor.

She trembled but she tried to put on a confident front. 'Are you sure about that?'

'Yes, I'm sure. The last thing you want is to make an enemy out of me.'

She barked out a harsh laugh. 'I think it's too late for that, don't you? What you just suggested is, well, it's barbaric. Sam is just a baby. She needs me.'

'Yes, she does.'

'She's too little to—' She stopped, gasped, then said slowly, 'Say that again.'

Alex stared back at her. 'I agreed with you. You are her mother. Of course she needs you. I never said that she didn't.'

She blinked, and breathed deeply. 'But you just said you'd sue me for custody.'

'And I meant it.' For the first time since he'd arrived at the apartment, Alex looked angry, his face hardening and nostrils flaring. 'Did you listen to yourself just now? Talk about being selfish. Have you thought for one moment that Sam needs me as much as she needs you? Have you?'

Katrina flinched. 'I've already said that—'

Alex didn't let her finish. He put his face close to hers and bared his teeth. His eyes were emitting blue sparks, his hands clenching and unclenching at his sides. 'My daughter is going to have a better start in life than I had; I can promise you that. She is *not* going to be raised in some dingy two-bit apartment barely big enough to swing a cat in. She is *not* going to go to bed hungry two out of three nights because there's not enough money to put a proper meal on the table. She is *not* going to be bullied, and she is *not* going to be scared.'

Alex stopped.

Katrina thought he'd finished but he'd only paused long enough to draw breath.

'She is going to have ballet and music and tennis lessons if that's what she wants. She is going to have friends and go to parties and not be embarrassed because she wears clothes that come from the cheapest chain-stores or other kids' hand-me-downs. She is going to feel safe and secure and happy. And I, as her father, am going to see that it happens. And to hell with anyone who gets in my way!'

CHAPTER FIVE

His words hung in the air like a crack of rifle fire, bouncing off one wall and then another before slowly echoing into nothing. The silence that invaded the room prickled at the back of Katrina's neck and made her skin contract over her bones.

As if sensing the tension in the room, Samantha started crying again. Katrina eased her grip, which had unconsciously tightened with each and every word that had exploded from Alex's mouth.

Laying the baby in the crook of her arm, she swayed from side to side.

The rocking motion soothed Samantha, who grew quiet.

It failed, however, to calm Katrina's own shattered nerves.

She was stunned by Alex's outburst. Not only was the sudden flare-up out of character, but the content had knocked her for six.

She knew next to nothing about Alex's family. When they'd been together he'd never talked about them. She knew his mother was still alive, because she'd called him several times, leaving messages he'd always ignored. She also knew he had a brother and, courtesy of the conversation she'd overheard between Alex and Dr Kershew that day in his surgery, she knew that his name was Michael.

Alex had never mentioned his father. Or his background.

She'd always assumed he came from a wealthy family. She didn't have a particular reason for thinking that; she'd just never associated a man who owned and ran his own investment bank with anything but success and wealth.

But his tirade just now had been full of such passionate intensity there was no doubt he was speaking from personal experience.

Tears stung the back of her eyes when she realised *he* was the little boy who had gone to sleep hungry. *He* was the little boy who had been bullied and scared.

'I'm sorry,' she said, looking up.

His jaw squared. 'What for? For the fact that I had a lousy childhood? Or the fact that you want to deny Sam everything I can offer her?'

Katrina bit back a gasp.

Alex was not holding back. The gloves were well and truly off.

Every word was like a sword he was thrusting through her—and each and every one found its mark.

'That isn't fair,' she protested, even though she knew there was a lot of truth in what he'd just said.

She'd contacted Alex for many reasons—included amongst them was the fact that she knew he could offer their daughter more financially than she could.

She had to face it, she was struggling. All she had to

do was look at the pile of unpaid bills pinned to the fridge door with magnets to see that she was just scraping by. She didn't want to see her daughter suffer that way.

'And is it fair that I get only the scraps from the table and not the full feast, which is exactly what I'd be getting if Sam lives with you?'

Katrina winced as that shot also found its target. 'I suppose not.'

'I have as much right to custody as you have.' His eyes met hers squarely. 'The difference is, I have the money to win.'

He was right.

Alex could afford the best legal counsel in Australia. In fact, he could hire a whole team of lawyers if he wanted to, whereas she would have to make do with legal aid.

It wouldn't be a fair contest. It would be over before it had even begun.

Her shoulders slumped, the energy draining out of her. 'OK. You win; I'll move in with you. But I won't sleep with you.'

His eyes seared into hers. 'I am *not* signing on for a lifetime of celibacy!'

She clenched her hands into fists. 'Well, don't think I'm just going to stand by while you sleep with other women!' she burst out before she could stop herself. 'I refuse to be humiliated that way,' she added hastily just in case he thought she was jealous.

Because she wasn't. Was she...?

Katrina was very much afraid that she was—and she didn't like it one little bit.

The look Alex threw her chilled her to the bone. 'What kind of a man do you take me for?' he demanded.

'Do you really think I'd risk doing anything that would hurt or embarrass my daughter if she found out?'

Katrina was ashamed to realise that she hadn't given a thought to how such behaviour would affect Samantha. She'd been too busy worrying about how *she* felt about it.

'I hadn't thought of that,' she admitted grudgingly.

'Well, I have. You either move in with me with the aim of building a proper family with all that that entails, or you don't move in at all.'

Her heart started to thump again. She now knew exactly what the saying 'between a rock and a hard place' meant. She was sandwiched between the two right now.

'You can't just expect me to jump straight into bed with you,' she huffed.

Alex shrugged. 'I don't see why not. It's not as if you haven't slept with me before.'

His insensitivity made her grit her teeth. 'It's not the same, and you know it. I didn't dislike you then the way I do now. I need time. Time to establish a relationship first.'

'We already have a relationship, or are you forgetting the fact that we spent almost a year together?'

Katrina's heart sank to her toes. 'I've forgotten nothing. That's the problem.'

In the end they agreed to a compromise.

Her move to the penthouse was completed with the minimum of fuss the following day. Alex arranged everything; the transfer happened with a speed that made her head spin.

After giving her a quick tour of the apartment, which

was as spacious as it was luxurious, Alex departed for the office. 'I'll be back around eight to see how you're settling in.'

Katrina was surprised he'd left so quickly. But then, she reasoned, he was a busy man who'd obviously taken time out of his schedule to be here to welcome them.

Alex had arranged to give her furniture away to charity, so it didn't take her long to unpack her meagre possessions. Even with her belongings scattered around her room, and a few favourite ornaments and photographs carefully positioned in the lounge, the apartment still didn't feel like home.

She'd never lived in anything so lavish, not even for a night. She felt like a fish out of water and, as a result, found it difficult to relax. So much so that she could hardly wait to put Samantha in her pram and go outside.

After a long walk down to Circular Quay, Katrina returned to the apartment and proceeded to put the baby to bed. The familiar routine of feeding and bathing her daughter was soothing.

Alex arrived home just before eight. Katrina was watching TV and pretending not to watch the clock at the same time.

'Have you eaten?' he asked, pulling off his tie and unbuttoning the collar of his shirt.

Katrina shook her head. 'No. Not yet.'

He undid another button. And another. Katrina tried not to stare, but found her eyes straying to the triangle of golden skin he'd revealed.

'Do you still like Chinese?' Alex asked, his fingers working the next button free.

By this stage half of his muscled chest was bare.

Alex looked good naked; his body was taut and toned. Katrina took full advantage of it before she realised he was waiting for her reply.

Dragging her eyes back to his face, she nodded.

'There's a list of restaurants in the third drawer down in the kitchen. Why don't you call the Chinese and order while I have a quick shower?' he suggested, pulling the open shirt out of the waistband on his trousers.

Katrina forced herself not to look down, even though the temptation to do so was strong. Was he doing this little striptease deliberately? she wondered, dragging in a breath before releasing it slowly. 'Fine. I'll do that.'

Alex shrugged off the shirt and let it dangle off one finger. 'Good. I shouldn't be long.'

'Do you have any preferences?' she choked out.

He flashed her a smile that made her go weak at the knees.

'You choose. You know what I like.'

He turned and walked out of the room.

Katrina stared at the strong planes of his back. She did know what he liked—and she wasn't just thinking about food!

She remembered several memorable occasions when they'd showered together, taking it in turns to wash each other. There was something very sensual about the combination of soap, water and skin that brought her out in goose bumps just thinking about it.

The Chinese food arrived not long after Alex had opened a bottle of crisp white wine. Katrina cautiously dished the food up on to the expensive china plates she'd found in the kitchen.

'One of these days you're going to have to master the art of using chopsticks,' Alex mocked as she picked up her fork.

Her mouth twisted. 'I've tried, but more food ends up in my lap than in my mouth.'

'I know. Do you remember the night I tried to teach you to use them?'

Katrina's eyes met his, the memory of that evening washing over her.

Alex had decided that a penalty-and-reward system would help her to learn more quickly.

Her reward had been a kiss. Her penalty had been the loss of an item of clothing.

She hadn't learned how to use chopsticks that night; she didn't think they'd even finished their meal. But she'd learned a lot about herself and about the depth of her desire for Alex.

Heat flooded her insides until she found it difficult to sit still. 'Don't, Alex. You promised you'd give me time.'

Alex shook his head. 'No, I didn't. I said I was willing to let our relationship progress naturally. There's a big difference.'

Katrina was beginning to realise that. 'I should have known better than to trust you. I thought you meant I could set the pace.'

'I'm not waiting until hell freezes over, if that's what you're thinking. I expect there to be progress.' He gave her a wicked smile. 'And I never said that I wouldn't give the pace a nudge along every now and again, did I?'

'Alex…'

He held up his hands, his electric-blue eyes wide and innocent. 'All we're doing is talking.'

'Is that what you'd call it? I'd call it a trip down memory lane.'

That nudge he'd just mentioned was also a blatant attempt to seduce her with memories.

Alex took a sip of wine before answering. 'And what's wrong with that? I see nothing wrong with re-connecting with our past. We used to have some pretty good times, if you remember.'

That was the problem.

She *did* remember. And she'd rather she didn't.

She remembered their first meeting in her boss's office, where one look from the tall, dark-haired, blue-eyed stranger had left her both breathless and speechless.

She remembered their first kiss that very same evening, when she'd trembled in his arms as if she'd never been kissed before.

But she also remembered each and every time he'd returned to his apartment, leaving her with the smell of him on her skin, the taste of him in her mouth and only the lingering heat of his body to keep her warm.

She looked him in the eye. 'Yes, we had some good times. But it wasn't all a bed of roses. At least, not for me.'

Alex frowned. 'Are you saying I made you unhappy?'

Katrina swallowed. 'Not entirely. I'm just saying I wasn't particularly good mistress material.'

His eyes narrowed to slits of blue. 'You wanted more than I could give you.'

It was a statement, not a question. Her fork clattered down on to her plate. 'You knew?'

He nodded. 'Although you didn't say anything,

you weren't very good at hiding your feelings. I warned you in the beginning that I didn't plan on getting married or having children. You should have listened to me.'

She inclined her head, an empty feeling attacking her insides, draining her of warmth. 'You're right. I should have. The point I'm trying to make is that I don't want to keep revisiting the past. If we're going to make this work we should start afresh.'

'Considering we have a daughter together, don't you think it's a little too late for that?'

She gestured with one hand. 'You know what I mean. Can't we just be friends for now? Until…you know… we get used to each other again?'

Alex looked as though the idea was totally alien to him, and Katrina guessed he'd never had a platonic relationship with a woman in his life. 'We're meant to be building a lasting relationship.'

'Then friendship is an excellent place to start, don't you think?'

'I don't know if that will work.' He picked up his wine and took a sip before saying slowly, 'You can't just pretend we don't want each other, Katrina. It won't make it go away.'

Picking up her fork, Katrina skewered a honey king-prawn and doggedly began eating without giving him a reply.

Alex obviously got the message, because he sighed and picked up his chopsticks.

'Are your rooms OK?' he asked a couple of minutes later.

He'd put her and Samantha in adjoining rooms with

their own bathroom. Her bedroom was large, spacious and luxuriously appointed.

Their daughter's bedroom had already been furnished as a nursery, complete with animal motifs on the walls and a pile of toys that must have cost a bomb.

'They're fabulous. How did you manage to decorate the nursery so fast?'

His mouth twisted. 'Money talks. I'm glad you like it.'

She smiled with genuine warmth. 'How could I not like it? It's fantastic. And whoever chose the toys did a wonderful job. Sam already loves the pink teddy-bear.'

Alex looked away, seemingly fascinated by the rice he'd picked up with his chopsticks.

Instinct prompted her to ask, 'Who bought the toys, Alex?'

He looked up somewhat sheepishly. 'I did.'

'I see.'

Katrina was stunned. Although why she should be she didn't know. Alex was nothing if not thorough; when he did things he went all out, crossing every t and dotting every i.

'I wanted to get Sam something from me,' he said in that same sheepish tone. 'I guess I got a little carried away, didn't I?'

She gave him a warm smile. 'Maybe just a little bit. You bought enough toys to last her until she's five. I don't want her spoilt.'

Alex smiled back. 'I don't want her spoilt either. I'll try not to get so carried away in future.'

Katrina's heart turned over, then wrenched hard.

This was so difficult.

Alex had virtually blackmailed her into moving in

with him. Now that she was here, she had two choices: she could either be as uncooperative as possible—in which case Alex would sue for custody and she would lose her baby—or she could try and make their relationship work, knowing it was the best thing for Samantha.

Obviously, she'd chosen the latter.

But—and it was a big but—she didn't want her emotions to become involved. That was easier said than done; Alex was pretty hard to resist when he turned on the charm.

After dinner they cleared the table. Katrina stacked the dishwasher and was about to retire to her room when Alex suggested she join him in the lounge for another glass of wine.

'There are a couple of things I want to discuss with you,' Alex added persuasively.

'Fine. I'll just check on Sam.' She hesitated and then asked, 'Do you want to come with me?'

He nodded.

Their daughter was sleeping peacefully in her cot, her fan-like lashes soft against her cheek.

'Is there anything more innocent or more wonderful than a sleeping baby?' Alex whispered.

Katrina shook her head. 'No.'

She reached in and straightened the covers then moved aside to allow Alex some space.

He brushed a gentle hand over the top of Samantha's head before stroking a finger down her cheek.

Returning to the lounge, Katrina sat down and folded her hands in her lap. 'What did you want to talk to me about?'

'A couple of things. First, transport.' Alex dug into his pocket and came out with a set of keys. 'Here, take these.'

'What are they?' she asked, automatically reaching out to take them.

'They belong to the silver BMW I had delivered for you this afternoon.'

Katrina put the keys down on the glass-topped coffee table as if they were a hot potato burning a hole in the centre of her palm. 'I don't need a car.'

'Of course you do. I don't want you relying on taxis. You need your own transport to get to and from appointments.'

A car was a luxury she hadn't been able to afford. The little second-hand sedan she'd owned before falling pregnant had been sold to help pay for all the additional expenses that went along with having a baby.

Since Samantha had been born, Katrina had used public transport to get around, just like thousands of other mothers did every day. It was no mean feat, considering all the gear she had to take everywhere with her, but it was adequate.

'I really don't think it's necessary. I'm quite happy to make do with public transport.'

Alex frowned. 'I had to *make do* when I was growing up. My daughter doesn't. I don't want you relying on public transport. End of story.'

Katrina wasn't happy with the way Alex had just laid down the law. She opened her mouth to argue and then quickly shut it again.

Alex had as much right as she did to have a say where their daughter was concerned. And she had to admit that a car would certainly make life easier. At the same time, she was conscious of the expense.

'OK, if you feel that strongly about it. But a BMW

isn't necessary. Any old second-hand car would be just fine for our needs. Is it too late to return it?'

'Yes, it is too late. I've already paid for it. Besides, I don't want to return it. I bought a BMW in the first place because it has an excellent safety record; that still stands. I want something that will protect you both in case of an accident.'

Katrina was warmed by his concern, even though she knew she was going to be terrified driving such an expensive car. 'Fine. If that's what you want.'

'It is. Now, to funds.' He handed her a yellow envelope. 'I've opened two credit cards in your name. Both have a five-thousand-dollar limit, so don't go berserk.'

Katrina shook her head. 'No. No way.' Even before she'd finished speaking, she'd placed the envelope down on the coffee table and pushed it towards him.

'Yes way. You're going to have to buy things for Sam,' Alex said smoothly. 'Prams. Car seats. Clothes. It will all add up. You'll also have your own expenses. I'd prefer it if you didn't return to work, so it's only fair that I support you.'

Katrina straightened her spine. She might have given in over the car, but this was another thing entirely. 'First, I have no plan to give up work. The company I worked for while I was pregnant agreed to take me back part-time after my three months' maternity leave is up. And—'

Alex frowned. 'You worked while you were pregnant?'

Katrina nodded. 'Of course.'

'There's no "of course" about it. You should have been taking it easy.'

'I was pregnant, Alex, not sick. I've always worked; I wouldn't know what to do with myself if I didn't. And

I didn't really have much choice. Having a baby is an expensive business; I had to work to pay the bills. Besides, I wanted to keep busy.'

In those first few months, she'd been agonizingly miserable.

One minute she'd been so angry with Alex she'd half-expected steam to pour from her ears. The next minute she'd been so hurt she'd burst into floods of tears.

No doubt pregnancy hormones had made her feel worse than she might otherwise have felt, but she'd been pretty low to start with.

Working had helped take her mind off Alex. It had also helped her to stop feeling so sorry for herself.

'I'm sorry I wasn't there to help,' he said grimly.

Katrina opted not to respond to that comment. They'd already had this discussion. Going over it *ad nauseum* wasn't going to help anybody.

'Second, I'm not a huge fan of credit cards,' she said, returning to the original conversation. 'My mother always said that if you can't afford to pay for it now you can't afford it at all.'

An odd look crossed his face that she couldn't quite decipher. 'I can assure you we can afford to use credit cards. But if you give me the details of your bank account I'll also transfer some cash to you each month.' He raised a hand. 'Don't say it. I have the right to share the expense of raising my daughter.'

Katrina snapped her mouth closed. She wanted to argue with him, but knew that he was right.

'Lastly, I wanted to discuss the household arrange-ments. I have a housekeeper who comes in three times a week. Her name is Leslie. She takes care of everything. Washing, cleaning and shopping. If you want to change those arrangements, feel free. I'll leave it up to you to sort out with her. I've told her about you and Sam. She's due here tomorrow around ten. I take it you can introduce yourself?'

Katrina wasn't quite sure what to say. She wasn't used to having household staff, nor did she think she wanted to get used to it. Given the choice, she would rather look after their home herself. But it was obviously an arrangement that suited Alex, and she didn't feel it was right to make waves so soon after arriving.

Suppressing a sigh, she inclined her head. 'Yes. No problem.'

'Now there are just a few logistical matters to take care of.'

Katrina couldn't think of another thing. Alex had taken care of everything with his usual thoroughness and efficiency. 'Such as?'

'Contact numbers.' He extracted a business card from his pocket. 'This has all of my numbers on it. Give me your mobile number so I can contact you when you're out. I think it's really important we keep each other posted about any plans we make. For example, I sometimes have business commitments in the evenings. If I'm going to be out, I'll let you know,' Alex said. 'Otherwise, I suggest we eat together.'

Katrina didn't know whether to welcome the suggestion or not.

She had enjoyed this evening.

If the truth be known, she'd enjoyed it rather more than she should have. This was only her first night here, and already she was fantasising about what it would be like if this was for real. Imagining what it would be like if they were a real family.

A family where she loved Alex and he loved her.

But there was no point building sandcastles in the air.

Alex thought love was an overrated emotion.

And she…

Well, she had lost her heart to Alex once. She had no intention of making the same mistake twice.

CHAPTER SIX

DURING the next few days they fell into a routine. But it was a routine Katrina wasn't the least bit happy with.

She wasn't quite sure what she'd been expecting when she'd agreed to move in with Alex, but it hadn't been this.

She hardly saw Alex. He left the apartment before she got up in the morning and often returned after she'd gone to bed.

The few times she had seen him, he'd been polite but distant. The easy camaraderie they'd shared on her first evening felt like a distant memory.

By the time the fourth night arrived, Katrina had had enough. Her distress wasn't personal, of course; she was upset on her daughter's behalf. Frankly, the less she saw of Alex the better.

But the situation couldn't go on. The only way to resolve it was to stay up and talk to Alex.

Her plan went skew-whiff, however, when she fell asleep.

She woke when strong arms lifted her.

'What the—?' she gasped, jerking awake.

Blue eyes stared down at her. 'You fell asleep.'

'Did I?' She yawned and pushed the hair back off her face. 'What time is it?'

'Eleven-thirty.'

'My goodness! I've been asleep for hours.'

'Have you?' His voice was husky.

Katrina nodded and blinked sleep drenched eyes. She was all too conscious of being cradled against the hard wall of his chest with his heat and all-male smell wrapped seductively around her. Desire flared low in her belly, her heart picking up rhythm.

'You can put me down now,' she suggested softly.

Alex let her legs swing gently to the ground, but he didn't immediately release her. He smoothed a strand of hair back behind her ear, and her stomach clenched at the fierce intensity burning in his eyes. 'I have to kiss you,' he said hoarsely.

He bent his head towards her. She had plenty of time to stop him, but she didn't.

She tried to tell herself that she didn't turn her head away because she was still only half-awake but she wasn't sure she was telling the entire truth.

It wasn't just the fuzziness of half sleep holding her captive. It was anticipation.

Alex claimed her with his mouth, softly at first and then with more intensity, prising her lips apart.

Even though she knew she shouldn't, Katrina closed her eyes and kissed him back.

When he raised his head they were both breathing heavily.

For a moment neither of them spoke.

Desire pulsed softly in the airwaves between them. It was a soundless beat that connected them in a way it was impossible to explain. And the power of it was impossible to ignore.

Katrina knew that if she didn't break the link soon she'd be all but inviting Alex to make love to her.

She had to admit she was tempted. But then she remembered why she'd been waiting up for him in the first place and the spell was broken.

Clearing her throat, she stepped backwards. The arm wrapped around her waist tightened.

Katrina pushed her hands against his chest. 'Let me go, Alex. We need to talk.'

His spare hand cupped her jaw, his thumb tracing the outline of her mouth. 'I'd much rather kiss you again.'

'And I'd rather you let me go,' she said quietly.

Alex searched her face. What he saw must have convinced him she meant what she said, because he sighed and released her. He wiped a hand over his face. 'OK. But before we talk I need something to eat.'

Katrina suddenly noticed how tired he looked. 'Haven't you had dinner?'

He shook his head. 'I didn't get a chance to. One of the big deals we've been working on went right off the rails today. Someone didn't do their job properly.' The hard edge sharpening his voice suggested the culprit had been severely dealt with. 'We spent the evening thrashing out a solution which we'll present to the client tomorrow.'

'I see.' She hesitated before tentatively suggesting, 'Would you like me to make you something?'

He nodded. 'If you don't mind. My usual effort is a sandwich.'

'I think we can do better than that,' she said, leading

the way into the modern kitchen. 'How does an ome-
lette sound?'

'Sounds great.'

Katrina opened the fridge door and pulled out eggs,
bacon, cherry tomatoes, capsicum, baby spinach and
cheese.

'Is there an open bottle of white in there?' Alex asked
from behind her.

She looked in the fridge door. 'Yes.'

She put it on the central bench and pushed it across
to him.

He raised a brow. 'Care to join me in a glass?'

Katrina shook her head. 'It's a little late for me.'

Alex poured a glass of wine and sat on a stool on the
other side of the work bench. 'You said you wanted to
talk to me. What about?'

Katrina broke three eggs into a glass jug and began
whisking them. 'It sounds kind of silly now.'

'It was obviously important enough to keep you up.'

She nodded and took a deep breath. 'It's just that I've
hardly seen anything of you since we moved in.' She
gave him a sheepish look before picking up the pepper
grinder. 'I was beginning to think you were avoiding us.
I realise now you've obviously just been very busy.'

Alex was silent for such a long time that Katrina
looked up.

Their eyes met.

Alex grimaced. 'Not entirely.'

Katrina raised an eyebrow.

'I'm always busy but the deal I was telling you about
earlier only exploded today. Before that…' He grimaced
again. 'Well, let's just say you weren't completely wrong.'

Surprise made her heart leap in her chest. She laid the knife she'd been using to chop the vegetables down on the cutting board. 'You mean you were avoiding us? But why? I don't understand.'

His eyes dropped to her mouth, where they lingered like a physical caress. 'Can't you guess?'

Her colour rose. His implication was clear. 'I…' She trailed off, scrambling for an appropriate response.

'I'm not used to going without something I want.' Alex picked up his glass of wine and took a sip. 'I thought it was prudent to stay out of your way for the time being. I thought it would be less frustrating.' His mouth twisted. 'Not that it's entirely worked.'

Katrina pressed her hands against the granite bench-top, welcoming the coolness against her heated skin. 'I…I don't know what to say.'

'Then don't say anything.' He raised an eyebrow. 'Unless you're ready to change your mind and come to bed with me.'

When Katrina shook her head and looked away, Alex sighed. 'I didn't think so.'

He was resigned to the fact that Katrina was going to make him kick his heels for several weeks before letting him into her bed. Her reasoning was a whole lot of gobbledegook that didn't make a lot of sense to him.

OK, he'd treated her badly. He was the first to admit that his behaviour had been appalling.

But she still wanted him—whether she wanted to admit it or not.

What was the point in making them wait? Frankly, he couldn't see any.

And while he was prepared to give her a bit of leeway he didn't plan on waiting for for ever. Maybe it was time to remind her of that.

'Just be aware that I won't let the current state of affairs continue for too much longer,' he warned softly.

Katrina, who now had her back to him as she busied herself at the stove, swung around. 'And what, pray tell, do you mean by that?'

Alex wasn't the least fazed by her snippy attitude. 'The situation will come to a head at some point. When it does, I won't take no for an answer.'

Her chin angled. 'Yes, you will. Otherwise it will be rape.'

Alex scowled at her. 'I've never had to force a woman to share my bed and I'm not about to start now. When the time comes, you'll be more than willing...you'll be begging me to take you.'

'I don't think so. You'll be lucky to even get to first base if you keep on avoiding me. The whole idea of waiting is so that we can establish a relationship before we sleep together. I need to learn to trust you again. I can't do that if I never see you.' She waved her spatula through the air. 'And have you even given a thought to the fact that by avoiding me you're also avoiding Sam?'

Alex frowned at her. 'I always pop into the nursery before I leave in the morning and again before I go to bed. I see Sam every day.'

'I didn't know that.' She turned to the stove, stirred the eggs for a moment and then swung back to him. 'But it's still not good enough. Not by a long shot. Sam's asleep then. I thought you said you were going to accept your responsibilities. But if you're not willing to make an effort to spend time with your daughter when she's awake then you're honouring diddley-squat!'

Alex immediately took offence. His glass landed on the granite bench-top with enough force to almost shatter it.

His father had neglected many of his responsibilities and had out-and-out abused others. The accusation Katrina had just thrown at him was totally unjustified. Couldn't she see how much effort he'd gone to to make sure his daughter was well provided for?

'How can you say that?' he demanded, his back ramrod straight. 'Sam has wanted for nothing since you moved in here. The second hand pram and capsule you had her in have been replaced by new ones. She has a wonderful nursery and heaps of toys. Everything that money can buy.'

She glared at him. 'This isn't about money. Or things. This is about love.'

'You know my opinion of that emotion,' he bit out coldly.

Her eyes grew so wide they dominated her face. 'I thought you were talking about your feelings regarding women—not your own flesh and blood.'

'Love is just a word that in and of itself means nothing. It's usually used as a substitute for something else. Between men and women, that something is usually lust. With familial relationships, it as often as not represents a combination of liking and respect.' He gave her a hard look. 'Sam will, without a doubt, have those things from me.'

'Well, you can't hope to bond with her on any level

if she's not even awake when you see her,' Katrina shot back at him, each word like a weapon she was using against him.

She really was Little Miss Confrontational these days, particularly where Samantha was concerned. 'That will happen in time. It's only been a couple of days.'

'Well, just remember that they are a couple of days you can never get back.' Katrina stared him in the eye, her face serious. 'Babies grow and develop so quickly; Sam has already changed so much since she was born. You'll both be missing out if you don't start spending time with her.'

Alex topped up his wine. In truth, he had been avoiding Samantha as much as he'd been avoiding Katrina—not that he intended to tell Katrina that. Nor did he intend to explain why he had been avoiding their daughter.

For the first time in years, the nightmares were back. Dreams of incidents from his past.

Some were of real beatings he'd been on the receiving end of. Beatings that had damaged his body but never his spirit.

Others were of his younger brother being similarly abused—despite Alex's attempts to stop it from happening.

Each image was so real it felt as if it had only just happened. Each vision was so authentic that he broke out in a cold sweat and woke trembling.

He knew why the dreams were back, of course—because he'd just learned that he was a father.

Now he had to face his greatest fear: that lurking somewhere inside him was the same monster that had lived inside his father.

Rationally, Alex knew he would never deliberately

hurt any child, least of all his own, in the way his father had taken pleasure in doing.

But what if he hurt Samantha through thoughtlessness or ignorance? What if he lost his temper and lashed out without thinking?

He'd done that once before, many years ago.

The thought of it happening again terrified the life out of him.

He would rather cut off an arm or a leg than hurt a single hair on Samantha's head.

But Katrina was right. There had to be a middle ground. Somewhere where he could build a relationship with his daughter at the same time as keeping her safe.

'OK. You've made your point, Little Miss Confrontation. I'll make sure I spend more time with her. Satisfied?'

She nodded. 'Tomorrow is Friday. I presume you don't work at weekends?'

Alex shook his head. 'I usually spend a couple of hours reading reports and doing emails, but, no, I don't work all weekend.'

'Then you have no objection if I arrange a couple of family outings for us, then, do you?'

If the quickest way into Katrina's bed was to spend time with her, then Alex would willingly spend every spare minute there he possessed.

And this conversation with Katrina forced him to acknowledge that spending quality time with his daughter was something he *must* do.

He'd spent so much time focussing on the practicalities of Samantha's care that he hadn't given a thought to the relationship itself.

Mind you, that was hardly surprising. It was easy to forget what a real father-child relationship should be like when you'd never had it.

Not that that was excuse. He'd watched his friends with their fathers. He'd been envious of the way other fathers had played ball with their sons, and how they'd told stupid jokes and teased each other.

There and then, Alex made a vow to himself: he was going to be a better father than his dad had been.

He would do things with Samantha. Lots of things.

And what better way of doing them than with Katrina at his side?

She was as fiercely protective of their daughter as a lioness with her cub. Nothing would happen while she was around to prevent it.

Alex shook his head and smiled, anticipation making his heart beat strongly in his chest. 'No. I have no objection whatsoever. In fact, I'm looking forward to it!'

The following day Katrina had just started to undress Samantha in preparation for bathing her when a sound made her turn.

She found Alex standing in the doorway, watching them.

He was wearing one of his to-die-for suits and a dark tie dotted with tiny diamonds.

He looked way too handsome for his own good, and Katrina had to swallow before speaking. 'Alex. I didn't hear you come in. You're home early.' Glad of an excuse to take her eyes away from him, she turned back to her daughter. 'Look who's here, Sam. It's Daddy.'

'I took what you said last night seriously. And, since

I managed to put out the fire on that deal earlier than I'd expected, I thought I'd surprise you.' He splayed his hands wide. 'So here I am, reporting for duty.'

'Well, you're just in time for Sam's bath. Why don't you join us?' she suggested softly.

He nodded. 'OK. What do I have to do?'

Katrina smothered a smile at the way Alex had asked the question. He sounded so serious and industrious, as if he had an important job to complete and he was waiting for a list of instructions.

'Well, since you've never bathed a baby before, I'll take care of the actual washing.' Katrina kept her face serious and her voice sober. 'But you have two very important tasks.'

He raised an eyebrow. 'And they are…?'

'First, you need to quack.'

Alex stared at her as if her skin had just broken out in a series of multicoloured spots. 'Quack?'

Katrina nodded and pointed to the yellow rubber-duck already bobbing on the water. 'Yes, quack. Sam likes the rubber duck but she likes it even more when you make quacking noises.'

'Really?' He looked and sounded sceptical.

'Yes, really.'

'And the second task?'

She placed a hand on his arm and leaned closer. 'Relax. Don't forget, you're meant to be having fun.'

Alex stared at her for a moment before his mouth turned up at the corners. 'Am I taking this too seriously?'

'Uh-huh.' She nodded. 'You certainly are. But then, you're an over-achiever. I wouldn't have expected anything less from you.'

His eyes glinted metallic blue. 'You're mocking me.'

'Maybe just a smidge,' she said, holding up thumb and forefinger with barely a hair's breadth between them. 'I used to love bath time. I want Sam to enjoy it too. So we try to have fun, don't we, poppet?'

Samantha cooed her total agreement.

'I see,' Alex said, still not sounding totally convinced.

'My mother was usually in charge of bath times, so it was a special treat when my dad came home early and supervised. I had a whole heap of toys, and Dad had sounds for each and every one of them.' She wrinkled her nose at him. 'He set the bar pretty high so you have a lot to live up to.'

'That's just great,' Alex muttered, as if the pressure of expectation was riding on his shoulders. 'You've never mentioned your father. Where does he live?'

'Nowhere. He died in a work accident when I was little.'

Alex frowned. 'How old were you when your mother died?'

'Thirteen.'

'What happened to you then? You said you had no other blood relatives.'

Tension slithered inside her. 'I went into foster care.'

'I never knew that.'

Katrina shrugged. 'I don't talk about it much. They weren't the happiest years of my life.'

He touched her arm. 'I'm sorry.' He glanced at Samantha then back to her. 'That's another reason you pushed so hard to make me accept Sam as my daughter, isn't it?'

Katrina nodded. 'I'd had quite an idyllic childhood

up until then. But afterwards…' She shivered. 'I don't want Sam to have to go through that—ever!'

'She won't have to.'

'I know. Thanks to you.'

'There's no need to thank me. She's my daughter.' He cleared his throat. 'Now, enough of this serious talk.' He shrugged off his suit jacket and hooked it over the door knob. Pulling his tie free, he neatly folded it before slipping it into his trouser pocket. Finally, he rolled up the sleeves of his business shirt to the elbows. 'I'm ready. Let's do it.'

Katrina finished undressing Samantha and slid her into the water.

The baby cooed and smiled. Quickly, Katrina used the soft sponge to give Samantha a quick all-over wash and then said to Alex, 'OK. It's over to you.'

Alex moved closer. His body brushed up against the side of hers, and the smell of male skin mixed with soap invaded her nostrils.

Katrina wanted to move away but it wasn't feasible. Instead, she tensed her stomach muscles and tried to pretend that it wasn't Alex standing beside her.

Alex hesitated and picked up the duck. He gave her a sideways glance. 'I feel ridiculous doing this.'

Katrina conceded that he did look uncomfortable. 'You don't have to do it if you don't want to.'

He dragged in a breath. 'No, I'll do it.'

Again, Katrina smothered a smile. He sounded as thought she'd just asked him to swallow a tablespoon of particularly obnoxious medicine and was screwing up his courage to do so.

A few half-hearted and less than enthusiastic quacks

followed. Samantha appeared fascinated by the fact that it was her father wielding the duck, but a little unsure about the sound he was making.

Katrina touched his arm for a moment before quickly retreating. 'Relax, Alex. Just remember what you liked when you were a kid and do the same thing.'

'I didn't have those kinds of bath times.'

Katrina looked at him. 'What sort of bath times did you have?'

His eyes met hers for an instant, the expression in them sending a shiver running down and then up her spine. 'Not the fun kind.'

Her heart wrenched. Not only had he gone to bed hungry but he hadn't had fun bath-times. What else had he been deprived of? she wondered, her heart going out to him.

'Well, just imagine what you would have liked and do that instead,' she suggested lightly.

Alex looked back at the duck, studied it for a moment and then let out a quack that immediately made both Katrina and Samantha smile.

Later, Katrina would wonder whether that was the moment she started falling in love with him all over again.

He raised a brow. 'Better?'

She smiled with genuine warmth. 'Much better.'

Katrina was thrilled with the effort Alex was making. Coming home early had earned him a brownie point. Helping with Samantha's bath had earned him another.

There was just one down side to all this. She was seeing another side of Alex. A softer side that she hadn't seen before.

The problem with that was that it made Alex more attractive.

And that was the last thing she needed, because she was already finding him attractive enough.

'I never knew bath time could be so much fun. Or so wet,' Alex said ten minutes later as he looked down at his drenched shirt-front.

Katrina giggled. 'I hope you're not planning on blaming our daughter for that.'

'I certainly am,' he replied indignantly. 'If she didn't laugh every time I whizzed the duck through the water and made those waves, then I wouldn't have kept on doing it.'

'Well, I hope you don't intend being that enthusiastic all the time. I'm saturated.' She plucked at her buttercup yellow blouse which was plastered against her like a second skin.

'I don't know,' Alex said huskily. 'I rather like the wet look.'

In fact, he more than liked it. Katrina's shirt was not only sticking to her like glue, but the water had also made the material semi-transparent. Alex could see the outline of her low-cut cream bra and the texture of the lace running along the edge. He could also see the outline of her erect nipples at the centre.

Unable to resist, Alex tunnelled a hand beneath the fall of her hair, bent his head and kissed her.

He'd barely had a chance to do more than taste the sweetness of her lips before Katrina dragged her mouth from under his. 'Don't, Alex.'

'Why not?' he demanded.

Her eyes didn't meet his. 'Sam is getting cold.'

Because there was a grain of truth in Katrina's statement, Alex didn't argue. But before he let her go he looked her in the eye and said, 'The day is coming when you're going to run out of excuses.'

Her eyes flashed quick-silver and she tossed her head.

Without saying a single word she'd managed to convey—graphically—exactly what she thought of that suggestion.

How had he ever thought that Katrina was biddable? Alex asked himself.

She was about as docile as an atomic bomb.

For some reason he found that fact as arousing as he found it irritating.

He wanted to reach out and haul her into his arms. But he resisted the urge. 'I think you'd better take Sam and get out of here before my baser instincts get the better of me.'

He heard her breath catch, but she didn't move. She just stood there staring at him.

'You have until the count of three,' Alex warned softly. 'And then you'd better not tell me that I didn't warn you. One. Two…'

She scuttled from the room with Samantha, swaddled in a fluffy towel, still in her arms.

Alex dragged in a deep breath. And then another. Slowly his heartbeat returned to normal.

When he felt that he was under control he went through the door to the adjoining nursery. Katrina had just finished dressing Samantha in a pair of pyjamas dotted with pink, blue and yellow teddy-bears.

'What happens now?' he asked lightly.

'It's bed time. I fed her before she had her bath. She seems to prefer it that way.'

'Well, I'd better kiss her goodnight, then.' He stepped forward. Before Katrina had time to object, Alex closed his arms around both of them. 'Goodnight, Princess,' he whispered, brushing his lips across Samantha's forehead and then her cheek.

Sam cooed with pleasure.

The simple sound was as powerful as a sword being thrust through his heart.

Warm pleasure flooded his insides until he felt as if he was glowing.

Holding Katrina and Samantha in his arms felt so right. As if it was meant to be.

Although he wasn't a believer in fate—he preferred to think that a man controlled his own destiny—Alex embraced the feeling.

'Alex, let me go. I need to put Sam down.'

Alex looked down. Already Samantha's lashes were fluttering closed. Reluctantly, he let his arms drop to his sides and then stood watching as Katrina tucked their daughter into her cot.

Samantha was asleep the minute her head hit the pillow.

Katrina picked up what he presumed was a baby monitor and flicked the dial. 'Does she still wake through the night?' he asked, guiltily aware that this was yet another aspect of parenting he hadn't given a thought to.

'Yes. I've been feeding her twice during the night, but it's gradually dropping down to one.'

Alex frowned. 'That must be pretty tiring.'

She nodded. 'It is. But it won't last for for ever. You have to be philosophical about these things.'

'I suppose you do. Now, why don't we get changed

into some dry clothes and then you can tell me what you have planned for the weekend.'

'OK. It will take me a few minutes. I need to clean up the bathroom.' She wrinkled her nose at him but there was a twinkle in her eyes as she said, 'Someone I know got water all over the cabinet and the floor.'

'Oops. I think that's my cue to leave.'

As he left the room Alex felt satisfied by what had transpired in the last few hours.

He'd enjoyed the evening. He'd enjoyed it a lot more than he'd expected.

He had a good feeling about this. About Samantha— and Katrina. His two girls.

He smiled.

That had rather a nice ring to it. Now more than ever he knew he'd done the right thing. His two girls belonged with him.

CHAPTER SEVEN

WHEN Katrina entered the lounge, Alex was there before her. He was seated on one of several brown-leather couches, his long legs stretched out in front of him.

Gone was the business suit. In its place was a pair of worn denims that clung to his lean hips and powerful thighs, and a figure-hugging cotton sports-shirt in a shade of blue paler than his eyes. His hair was damp, as if he'd just had a shower, and his jaw had lost the end-of-day stubble he'd been sporting, suggesting he'd also shaved.

He looked gorgeous and sexy and way too attractive.

Alex saw her and smiled. It was a smile that pierced straight through her. 'I took the liberty of pouring you a glass of white wine. I hope that's all right?'

'That's fine. Thanks.'

Alex scooped up the glass from the coffee table and held it out to her. Katrina crossed the room and took it from his outstretched hand. Their fingers brushed and a tingle of electricity zapped up her arm.

She jerked, almost spilling the wine.

Alex frowned. 'Why are you so jumpy?'

She shrugged. 'I don't know. I'm probably just tired.'

Even as she said the words she knew they weren't true.

She was nervous. She knew it was stupid but she couldn't help it. Sharing Samantha's bath time with Alex made her feel as if she'd been suddenly stripped of all her defences.

It had started with their close physical proximity; it had been impossible to ignore the heat radiating off his body straight into hers. Impossible, too, to ignore the smell of his skin or the scent of his shampoo.

But what had really undone her was seeing the other side of Alex. She was used to Alex as he usually was. Confident. Controlled. Arrogant.

This evening, he'd totally disarmed her with his willingness to be teased and his eagerness to please Samantha and the hint of vulnerability he'd shown.

Alex patted the sofa beside him. 'Well, sit down for a while and relax.'

Katrina hesitated a moment before taking the seat opposite.

Alex frowned and put his wine glass down on the table with a clatter. 'This has to stop.'

Katrina clasped her hands around her glass. 'What does?'

He stared at her through narrowed eyes. 'Last night you accused me of avoiding you. Well, now it's my turn. I'm going to accuse you of doing the exact same thing.'

She folded her arms. 'You can hardly accuse me of avoiding you when we've spent the last hour together.'

'Actually, I can. You might be in the same room, but you're doing your best to prevent me getting close to you. Every time I touch you, you jump. Every time I kiss you, you come up with an excuse to stop me.'

'You said you'd let me set the pace,' Katrina protested.

'And I also said that I'd give the pace a nudge along every now and then. There is a halfway point, you know. Would it really have hurt you to sit beside me for a while? Maybe hold hands, share a couple of kisses?'

Katrina didn't want to answer him.

She didn't want to admit that she had stop him from doing those things because she was scared of what would happen if she didn't.

'You're meant to be trying but you're not,' Alex continued. 'You accused me of honouring diddley-squat but what about you?'

Katrina clenched her hands into fists at her side. 'I'm not the one who started this, Alex. You are. I can't just wave a magic wand and forget all the horrible things you said to me. It's not that easy.'

Alex sat forward and splayed his hands wide, forearms resting on his knees. 'What do you want me to say, Katrina? I *should* have believed you. I know that. I made the biggest mistake of my life when I said those things to you. And we've all paid for it.' His eyes seared into hers. 'I missed seeing you grow big with our child. I missed watching my daughter being born. As you pointed out yesterday, I can never get those things back.'

He paused but only to draw breath. 'And you. You were alone during your pregnancy and the birth. But it's not the same as having the father of your child with you during that special time. And Sam…? She went without a father for the first weeks of her life.'

'Alex—'

He held up a hand, his face gravely serious. 'No, let me finish. I want you to know that I haven't taken any of those things lightly. When I apologised to you, I wasn't just paying lip service. I wasn't going through the motions just for the sake of it. I apologised because I meant it.'

Katrina stared at him.

She didn't say a word. She couldn't. She was stunned by what Alex had just said, and how he'd said it.

His voice was so full of passion that each word had exploded inside her like a bomb detonating.

She had no doubt he meant every word.

'I can't undo the past,' Alex continued. 'But what I *can* do is work on the future. I'm willing to do everything within my power to make us a family. The question is, are you? Or are you so bitter that you can't ever forgive me? Because if that's the case then you should tell me—right here and right now—and we'll call it quits before we go any further.'

Katrina felt as though the bottom had just dropped out of her stomach and her world. A vacuum formed inside her; anxiety clutched at the back of her throat.

Much as she didn't want to admit it, there was a lot of truth in what Alex was saying.

She remembered the moment he'd apologised.

I'm sorry, he'd said.

And she, without a second's hesitation, had said, *apology accepted.*

Why? Because it had been the right thing to do— for Samantha.

But that had been the mother in her talking, the part of her that would do anything for her daughter—including swallowing her pride.

But she wasn't just a mother.

She was a woman too.

And the woman in her had been thinking that Alex's apology was way too little and way too late. The woman in her had clung to every little barb and every little jab of pain as if it were her lover.

Alex said he hadn't just been going through the motions when he'd apologised. Katrina was ashamed to admit that her acceptance of his apology had been exactly that: it had been expedient. A means to an end.

But, deep down, she hadn't forgiven Alex.

There was a ball of bitter resentment inside her that hadn't unravelled in the least. It was as tightly wound as the day it had formed.

She dragged in a breath then met his eyes squarely. 'There's some truth in what you said. I must admit, I didn't think your apology was genuine.'

'And now that you realise it was?'

She couldn't lie. She couldn't take something as pure as his honesty and as deeply felt as his regret and rip them to shreds. It would be like plucking the stars from the sky and trying to squash them under her heel.

'It…it makes a difference,' she said, unable to look away from him.

Already she could feel the ball of resentment and bitterness unravelling, as if it was made out of string and Alex had taken one end and was slowly pulling on it.

'Good.' The fact that he didn't hide his relief underlined the importance he was placing on their conversation. 'But is it enough? Is it enough to allow you to *really* put the past behind you and move forward?'

'I'm not sure,' she said honestly.

She hadn't had a chance to think that far.

She was confused, and scared. As if the world had spun into action and she was no longer sure of her place in it.

There had been a certain security in clinging to those bad memories. Hanging on to them had had the same effect as placing a protective barrier around her heart. They'd made her feel safe.

Realising Alex had meant every word of his apology had just torn that protective barrier to shreds. And spending the evening with him and Samantha had stripped her of her defences.

It was a double whammy that left her feeling exposed and vulnerable.

Alex leaned back against the sofa. Although his movement added only an extra foot to the distance between them, it suddenly felt like miles of wide, open space.

Suddenly, Alex felt as out of reach as a man on the moon.

And she...

Well, she felt very alone and isolated.

'Then I suggest you think about it,' he said in a cool, clipped voice. 'If you can't let go of the past, then we don't stand a chance. If you're not prepared to try, we're wasting our time.'

Her heart thumped. 'And Sam?' she asked, knowing what the answer would be but needing to hear it anyway.

'I told you before—I don't intend to give up my right to being a full-time father.' He sounded as determined as a bulldozer ploughing through a brick wall. 'Think about it: if you decide to call it quits now, everybody loses. You. Me. But most of all Sam.'

Katrina stared at him. Thoughts were spinning with fevered intensity through her brain.

Fear was beating on the inside of her skull.

If she pulled the plug, she would lose Samantha.

She'd rather cut out her heart than let that happen.

Alex sighed, heavily. 'Tell me something, Katrina. When you confronted me in the boardroom what did you hope to achieve?'

It was a good question. It was just a shame that she didn't have a good answer.

'I'm not sure.' She clasped her hands tightly together in her lap. 'I tried not to have too many expectations because I was afraid of being disappointed. Obviously, I wanted you to accept Sam and be a part of her life, but I hadn't thought as far as the practicalities of how we'd go about doing that.'

Alex stared at her for a long moment.

It felt as though he was looking right inside her. Into her mind. Her heart. Her soul.

'You keep on telling me this is about Sam. But do you know what I think? I think you're fooling yourself. If you were really putting Sam first you'd be going out of your way to make this relationship work instead of putting up obstacles at every opportunity. I don't think this is about Sam any more. This is about you. This is about your hurt feelings, your wounded pride.'

His words lingered in the room like the residue of gunfire, bouncing off one wall and then another. They rebounded inside her head with the same ferocity.

Because he was right.

It *was* about her and her hurt feelings.

It was about the things he'd said to her when she'd told him she was pregnant, and it was also about the fact that she'd loved Alex with all her heart and he hadn't loved her.

But more than anything it was about trying to avoid getting on the slippery slide of emotions that would lead to her falling in love with him all over again.

Alex could barely breathe as he waited for Katrina's reply.

He had handled this conversation like a rank amateur. For a man who negotiated multi-million-dollar contracts, and managed billions of dollars worth of investments, he had bungled one of the most important conversations of his life.

He'd pushed too soon.

It was a strategic mistake he never made when he was trying to land a big deal, but he'd made it now.

With every second that passed his stomach muscles grew more and more rigid and his throat felt as if invisible hands were squeezing around it.

All the while his eyes never left her face.

Finally, after what felt like for ever, her chin came up. She looked beautiful, proud, grave and serious. 'You're right. This is meant to be about Sam, but I've let my feelings get in the way. For that I apologise.'

The air rushed from his lungs so quickly he felt light headed.

He'd been half-convinced she was going to tell him their relationship would never work. That she would never be able to forgive him for the things he'd said to her.

What he'd have done then, he didn't have a clue.

He would not have wanted to take Samantha away from her mother, but nor would he have been prepared to abandon her.

It would have been an impossible choice—and one he was glad he didn't have to make.

And Katrina? Well, he wasn't prepared to let her go either.

She was the mother of his child. She was also the woman he wanted more than he thought it was possible to want a woman.

Relief and pleasure burst to life inside him.

'Apology accepted,' he said smoothly.

She raised a delicately plucked eyebrow. 'Just like that?'

He inclined his head. 'Just like that. As we keep on saying, this is about Sam. We've both forgotten that on occasion. We've let our feelings get in the way of what's best for her.' He stared at her, coiled tension strangling his insides. 'Can I take it you're prepared to give it a shot? To try to make *us* work?'

Anticipation held him still.

'I do want to make this work,' she started carefully.

'This…?' he prompted.

Her cheeks flushed with colour. '*Us*. My reasons for wanting both of us in Sam's life still stand. And I have to admit that providing Sam with a real family is by far the best thing for her.'

Alex sat as still as a statue for an entire minute, letting her words filter though his system.

Then he moved.

Rising to his feet, he rounded the coffee table until he was standing right in front of her. Reaching down, he grasped her hands and pulled her upright, straight into his waiting arms.

Her hands went to his chest. 'But that doesn't mean—'

Alex refused to let her go. His eyes drilled into hers. 'Yes. That's exactly what it means.'

'Alex—'

He kissed the words right out of her mouth. His mouth glided over hers, and one hand tangled in the silken length of her hair. Finally, heart pounding, he lifted his head. 'Doesn't it?'

Katrina stared at him. A mixture of emotions flitted across the surface of her eyes like scudding clouds. 'I don't think…'

'Don't think,' Alex whispered. His hand tightened in her hair, pulling her head back on the slender length of her neck. *'Feel!'*

And then he kissed her again. And again.

When he lifted his head Katrina was clutching his shirt front and her body was trembling against him.

He ran a hand over the soft silkiness of her hair. 'I'm going to make love to you,' he warned softly.

He gave her plenty of time to stop him.

But she didn't.

Alex didn't need a second invitation. He smoothed a strand of hair back behind her ear, his fingertips feathering against her cheek. He pulled her closer, so close the smell of female flesh wrapped seductively around him.

He bent his head and claimed her with his mouth, softly at first and then with more intensity, prising her lips apart.

This time when he lifted his head he rested his forehead against hers. 'I want you to be sure,' he whispered. 'If you're not, you'd better tell me now because in another minute or two it will be too late.'

For a heartbeat she didn't say anything.

Alex could hardly breathe. He didn't even think his heart was beating.

And then she smiled. 'I'm sure.'

Not saying a word—he didn't think he could utter a single syllable when she was looking up at him with desire-drenched eyes—he swung her up in his arms and carried her down the corridor.

He was almost at his bedroom door when he hesitated.

He'd always made it a practice to keep the women in his life out of his bed. It was a demarcation line that he had never crossed, a warning to his lovers that their position in his life was limited.

But Katrina was the mother of his child. She was the woman he wanted above all others.

She had just agreed to try and make their relationship work.

Surely those old boundaries had no place in his life any more?

'What is it?' Katrina asked when Alex hesitated in the hallway.

'Nothing.'

Instinctively, Katrina knew that it was far from nothing. In fact, her heart soared when he pulled open the door, the significance of the action not lost on her.

Alex had always found little—and sometimes big—ways of maintaining an emotional distance from her.

Keeping her out of his apartment, and thus out of his own bed, had been one of them. If she'd wanted a sign that he was committed to making their relationship work, he'd just given it to her.

They were both taking steps towards being a real family.

Some were baby steps. Others as significant as man landing on the moon.

Alex put her carefully down in the centre of the king-sized bed. Straightening, he began unbuttoning his shirt before shrugging it off and dropping it on the floor.

Katrina's mouth ran dry. Alex had a fantastic body, the result of daily jogging and strenuous gym sessions. She watched as his fingers went to his belt buckle.

She could hardly draw breath as Alex kicked his trousers aside, divested himself of his underpants and strode to the bed. Although his movements were economical rather than designed to arouse, Katrina couldn't take her eyes off him.

A pulse beat between her legs, and a dragging sensation pulled at her insides. Then she wasn't thinking at all as Alex came down on the bed beside her.

'Sit up,' he instructed, his voice rippling down her spine.

Katrina did as she was told, albeit shakily.

Alex stripped her of her clothes with a speed that left her reeling. When his eyes focussed on her naked breasts, they grew heavy, desire tightening their tips into prominent peaks.

'Back.' His voice was hoarse.

She did as she was told, this time collapsing back against the pillows, her breath coming in little gasps.

Alex looked at her. Just looked at her.

'I'd forgotten how beautiful you are,' he murmured, his voice feathering down her spine. 'You are truly magnificent.'

'So are you.'

He didn't answer her.

At least, not with words.

But his touch told her a lot.

He caressed her almost reverently, as if he were afraid she would disappear in a puff of smoke the minute he touched her.

His hand flattened over her abdomen and his eyes flashed to hers. 'What did you look like when you were pregnant?' he asked huskily.

Her breath hitched in the back of her throat. It was the last question she'd expected. 'Like most women, I suppose—big and fat.'

He shook his head. 'I bet you were stunning. I would have liked to have seen you swollen with my child.'

It was a beautiful thing to say.

Her heart swelled until it was fit to burst. She wasn't sure how to respond so she said nothing.

And then she wasn't capable of thinking at all as Alex bent his head and kissed her.

His hands and mouth were everywhere, fire and silk. He knew exactly what drove her to distraction. Knew what made her cry out loud with ecstasy—and what made her thrash against the pillow.

Unable to contain the sensations coursing through her, she dug her nails into his skin.

Alex lifted his head. 'Drawing blood again, are you, Kat?' he asked huskily, using the pet name he only ever used when they were in bed together.

Katrina smiled and dug them a little bit harder. 'Yes, I am. You'd better be careful you don't bleed to death.'

Surprised appreciation burst from his throat in laughter that soon turned to a groan as she took him in her hand and boldly stroked him. He left her side only long enough to ensure they were protected, then spread her trembling thighs and plunged inside her.

Katrina cried out. The feel of him filling and stretching her sent pleasure rolling through her in waves. She wanted to hang on to this moment for ever.

Alex froze as if she'd shot him. 'Did I hurt you? I didn't think. After the baby…'

'I'm OK.' She moved her hips in an upward motion that drew him in even deeper. 'More than OK.'

His frown turned into a sexy smile as he withdrew and thrust again. 'I can see that.'

They didn't talk any more after that. It was as if a spell had been woven around them, transporting them to a magical place where there was just the two of them, dominated by senses spinning out of control and hearts beating as one.

Alex threaded a strand of Katrina's hair through his fingers and let it drop on to the pillow. It felt like silk and looked like multi-coloured satin, moonbeams picking out strands of cinnamon, gold and honey.

The clock showed it was just gone one in the morning. He should be asleep. Why he wasn't, he had no idea.

He usually slept through the night without stirring—particularly after making love.

Maybe it was because this was the first time he'd shared his bed with a woman. He'd always thought he wouldn't like it. He enjoyed his own space, and was partial to sprawling across the sheets without having to worry about someone else getting in the way.

But waking and finding Katrina's soft, warm body wrapped around his had sent a shaft of pleasure through him.

He picked up another handful of hair and let it play through his fingers. This time some fell against her cheek. Softly, he stroked it back off her face.

Then, giving in to temptation, he reached down and pressed a kiss against the corner of her mouth. She murmured in her sleep and rolled towards him.

Alex wrapped his arms around her and kissed her again.

She blinked and opened her eyes. 'Alex.' His name was a sigh on her lips, a sigh that echoed inside him.

'No regrets?' he whispered.

She shook her head, and then she smiled at him. Not just with her mouth, but with her eyes. A hand reached inside his chest and squeezed tight. It was the way she used to smile at him. Alex didn't realise until that moment just how much he'd missed it.

'No regrets,' she whispered.

Satisfaction, and an emotion he couldn't quite define, swept through him. He rolled over so that she was half-lying beneath him. 'Good…because I want to make love to you again.'

She dug her fingers into his hair. 'I'm not stopping you.'

CHAPTER EIGHT

'DO YOU realise that's the first time Sam has slept right through the night?' Katrina said the next morning.

Alex brushed her hair aside then angled his mouth against the side of her throat. 'Obviously she realised that her parents had more important things to do.' His mouth slid lower, nibbling at the area where her neck met her shoulder. 'In fact, that's given me an idea.'

Katrina laughed. 'I can feel exactly what kind of an idea it's given you, and the answer is no. We can't right now.' To soften the blow, she turned in his arms, reached on to her tiptoes and pressed a kiss against his mouth. She'd forgotten how nice it was to touch him whenever she wanted to and kiss him whenever she felt like it. 'Our daughter needs feeding before she wakes the entire building.'

'You're right. You'd better attend to her before the neighbours call and complain. I'm going to have a shower.' Looking down at his body, he grimaced. 'I'd better make it a cold one.'

Katrina giggled.

Alex wagged a finger at her. 'You'll pay for that, young lady.'

'I'll look forward to it,' she said saucily.

Alex laughed.

Katrina was still smiling as she went in to the nursery. 'OK, missy, that will be enough out of you. Mamma's here to feed you.'

Reaching into the cot, she picked up her daughter and walked to the chair she reserved for feeding.

A couple of minutes later, Katrina looked down at her daughter suckling at her breast and realised that she felt happier than she had in a long, long time.

Even Samantha's birth, which should have been the most special, magical moment of her life, had been marred by the fact that Alex hadn't been there to share it with her.

For the first time, Katrina believed they had a future together. Before now she hadn't even dared to hope that it was even a possibility.

If there was one thing that could bridge the gap between them, it was their daughter. She was a unifying force that could just create a miracle.

'I think we're going to make it,' she whispered, stroking a hand down her daughter's back.

After dressing Samantha, Katrina went in search of Alex. The smell of frying bacon led her to the kitchen.

'I thought you said you couldn't cook,' she said, when she saw the feast he was preparing.

'Bacon and eggs isn't what I'd call *cooking*. All you have to do is shove them in the pan and make sure you get them out before they burn. Even I can manage that.' He turned and looked at Samantha. 'Good morning, Princess.'

Katrina put the bassinette down on the floor. 'Do you need a hand?'

'No. I have everything under control.'

Katrina watched Alex move confidently around the

kitchen. He had on the same worn denims he'd been wearing the previous evening, but this time he'd teamed them with a plain white T-shirt. Both clung in all the right places and Katrina couldn't stop her eyes from roaming over him.

'OK. We're ready,' he said, and put a plate piled high with food in front of her.

She laughed. 'I hope you don't expect me to eat all that.'

'Don't worry. I'll finish whatever you don't eat.' His eyes glinted. 'I happen to be starving this morning.'

Katrina flushed. She knew exactly what had given him such a healthy appetite.

Alex laughed. Then, obviously taking pity on her, he asked, 'So, how has your first week been?'

'After last night, how can I say that it's been anything but good?'

Alex grinned. It was a very boyish grin.

Like her, he seemed more relaxed. More at ease with the situation.

Last night they'd turned a corner. It wasn't just that they'd slept together; it went a lot deeper than that.

They'd addressed some important issues. Not only had they demolished a couple of stumbling blocks but they'd taken some positive steps forward.

For the time since she'd moved in, they really were a united team, working towards a common goal.

Katrina had to admit that it felt good.

'You're good for a man's ego.' The grin dropped from his face. 'But, seriously, how has it been? You have a new baby and a new home. You're going through some big adjustments. It would be quite normal for you to be feeling a little out of kilter.'

'I'm getting there. Settling into a routine has helped. But I must admit I feel as if I have too much time on my hands. I can hardly wait to get back to work.' She gave him an appealing look. 'Does that make me a bad mother?'

'Of course not,' Alex was quick to answer. 'But, speaking of your job, I'd like you to reconsider going back to work.'

Katrina just stared at him. 'Why?'

He shrugged. 'My mother had no choice but to work. She wasn't there when…' He raked a hand through his hair and around the back of his neck. 'Let's just say she wasn't always there when we needed her. I'd prefer it if Sam was your main priority.'

'Let's get something straight, Alex,' Katrina said, sitting up ramrod-straight. 'Sam is *always* my top priority. I can work and be a mother at the same time, you know. Just as *you* can work and be a father.'

'OK. Fair comment. But I'd really prefer one of us to be available all the time. At least until she's old enough to go to school. And, while I could be that person, it doesn't make sense financially.' He placed his hand over hers. 'I feel strongly about this. Please—will you at least think about it?'

Katrina unbent a little. At least he was asking her, not telling her. 'OK, I'll think about it. But I'm not promising anything,' she added quickly when she saw his smile. 'I really wouldn't know what to do with myself. I'm already struggling.'

His smile widened. 'Well, I might just have a solution for your boredom.'

Katrina grimaced as she cut into a crispy piece of bacon. 'Don't put it like that. It makes me sound as though I don't appreciate Sam, and I do. I love her to bits. She just doesn't completely fill my day.'

'You don't need to apologise. I completely understand. You're used to being busy; there's nothing wrong with that.'

'You said you might have a solution?' she asked hopefully.

He nodded. 'I do. In fact, I have a number of suggestions.'

'What are they?'

Alex gave her another of those boyish grins that made her heart turn over. 'I'm a big-shot executive, you know. I expect to be paid for my ideas.'

The look in his eyes made it perfectly clear exactly what kind of payment he was referring to.

Desire pooled low in her belly, her nipples tightening in the confines of her bra. 'Do you, now?'

His eyes glinted. 'Yes, I do.'

Katrina rose to her feet and went to brush past him. 'Well, I'd better go and get my purse. I'm sure I can spare twenty cents.'

Alex snagged her wrist and pulled her down onto his lap. 'Twenty cents? That's an outrage.'

'You're right.' Katrina nodded seriously. 'In the current financial climate, we should be watching our pennies. Let's make it ten cents instead.'

The tips of his fingers found the sides of her ribcage and tickled her.

Katrina writhed like an eel, her bottom grinding into his lap.

'Stop!' she gasped. 'I give up.'

Alex stopped wriggling his fingers and stared down

at her. 'You're going to have to pay for your insubordination, young lady. The price has just gone up. It's now going to cost you two kisses for each of my ideas'

She looked at him from under her lashes. In this mood, Alex was simply irresistible. 'I think I can manage that,' she murmured, her insides curling in anticipation.

His arms tightened around her. 'Well, pucker up, sweetheart. Here comes kiss number one.'

Katrina did as she was told and pursed her lips. His mouth landed softly on hers, lingered for just a moment and then retreated.

Her eyes blinked open.

'Now for kiss two,' he whispered huskily.

Her eyes fluttered closed again. This time his lips claimed her mouth with searing intensity. When he was done, he ran the tip of his tongue around the edge of her mouth before lifting his head.

'Just how many of these ideas do you have?' she whispered.

'A few.'

'Good,' she breathed.

Alex laughed. She could feel the rumble of his chest against her side.

He tapped her on the nose with the tip of his finger. 'OK. Pay attention now. Because I'm about to tell you about my first idea.'

'OK. I'm all ears.'

With his spare hand, Alex rubbed the side of his jaw. 'I've been thinking about this apartment.'

'What about it? It's gorgeous.' It was gorgeous— even if she did feel like she was living in a fancy hotel rather than a real home.

'But it's not exactly child-friendly, is it? It's OK for the moment. But as soon as Sam starts to walk it will be a disaster.'

Katrina looked through the open kitchen door at the miles of plush, cream carpet and the glass-topped tables and grimaced. 'You're right. In fact "disastrous" would be an understatement.'

'Which is why I'd suggest you start looking for a new house for us.'

Katrina struggled into a sitting position on his lap and stared him straight in the eye. 'Do you mean it?'

He nodded. 'I've been thinking about it ever since you moved in, but the time never seemed right to suggest it. I think it is now, don't you?'

The question was an acknowledgement of how much things had changed between them. Obviously Alex had been hanging back until their relationship was on a more stable footing. Now that they were both committed, he'd put his foot on the accelerator and was ready to go full steam ahead.

She nodded.

'I want something with a yard for Sam to play in, and maybe a swimming pool,' Alex suggested thoughtfully.

Katrina remembered his tirade the day he'd learned he was Samantha's father; he'd mentioned that he'd grown up in a small apartment without a yard to play in.

'I think that's a wonderful idea. Have you got an area in mind?'

'I was thinking about somewhere on the north shore. What do you think?'

'That's fine. Apart from the yard and the pool, do you have any other requirements?'

Alex started rattling off a list of criteria that made her head spin. 'Hang on a minute; I need to write this down.'

Scrambling off his lap, Katrina dashed through to her bedroom, rooted around in her handbag for her notepad-cum-diary and returned to the kitchen.

Sitting back down in her seat, she scribbled down a couple of things, asked Alex to repeat several others and dutifully added them to the list. Luckily, they had similar tastes, and most of what he'd suggested matched her requirements. 'What about budget?'

He named a figure that took her breath away. 'Now you've lost me.'

He frowned. 'What do you mean?'

'I was thinking of the kind of house I grew up in, which was a two bedroomed semi-detached cottage with a garage and a small yard. You're talking about something altogether different.'

'Not really. Just something bigger.'

'And grander,' she said, trying to keep her tone even.

'You don't like grand?' he asked, raising an eyebrow.

How did she answer that? 'I guess I'm not used to it. I want a home that…' She shrugged, not sure how to put her feelings into words. 'Well, something that feel like a *home* rather than a showpiece.'

'Can't it be both?'

'I suppose so,' she said doubtfully.

'I know so.'

Katrina sighed and chewed on the end of her pen. 'Wherever we buy, it needs to be reasonably close to schools too.'

'Which brings me to my next point.' Alex beckoned her with a finger and a come-hither smile that made her heart go crazy. 'But not without my payment. Come here.'

Katrina rose to her feet, a tingle of excitement rippling through her. Instead of sitting in his lap, she bent from the waist and pressed her mouth against his. Alex fed his hands into the hair on either side of her head and took control of the kiss.

Slowly, he withdrew his mouth from hers. 'One,' he breathed. 'Two,' he said, and plundered her mouth again.

By the time he lifted his mouth from hers, Katrina's legs were trembling so badly she was in danger of falling down. She staggered backwards and collapsed in her seat.

Neither said anything for a moment. Silence filled with the beat of desire wrapped around them.

Alex was the first to break it. He cleared his throat before speaking. 'I want Sam to go to the best school we can afford. I don't know a lot about how this works, but I should imagine we might have to put her name down somewhere quite early. Why don't you do some research into our options? If you come up with a shortlist we can register our intentions with a couple of schools.'

Katrina, who had been educated more than adequately in a state school, opened her mouth to argue but just as quickly shut it again. From previous comments, it was clear Alex's experience had not been as good as hers. If he wanted to send Samantha to an expensive school, then who was she to argue?

She picked up her pen and tapped the end on the table. 'Maybe I should look at schools first. It might influence where we decide to live.'

'Good idea.'

She snapped her diary closed. 'Well, that ought to keep me busy for a while.'

'I haven't finished yet,' Alex said smoothly.

Her eyebrows shot towards her hairline. 'What else is there?'

He looked at her with a glint in his eyes.

Katrina couldn't help it; she laughed. She held up her hands in mock surrender. 'I know, I know. Kisses.'

She propped her elbows on the table and leaned forwards. Alex met her halfway.

This time when they kissed only their mouths touched.

But that was enough. More than enough. When it was over they both collapsed back into their seats.

Katrina felt dazed, as if she'd been plugged into an electrical outlet and the power switched on to full voltage. There were so many sensations racing through her system she half-expected her hair to stand on end before emitting fiery sparks.

Alex appeared similarly affected, although he was the first to recover.

He raked a hand through his hair. His eyes were such a dark blue they appeared almost black. 'OK. Now, where was I? Yes, that's right; I almost forgot. I have a couple of functions coming up. I'd like you to attend them with me.'

Katrina dragged in a deep breath and tried to concentrate. 'What kind of functions?'

'They're business dinners—which brings me to my last suggestion.'

Katrina went to stand up but his next words stopped her. 'No, don't get up. I'll collect my payment afterwards. In bed.'

Anticipation burned a hole in her stomach. Excitement made a pulse beat at the apex of her thighs.

'OK. What is it?' she asked breathlessly.

'We're going to need some kind of childcare if you're going to attend functions with me.'

The suggestion caught her off-guard. If felt as though a bucket of cold water had just been poured over her. A hollow formed inside her. Her breath hitched in the back of her throat.

'I've never been separated from Sam before,' she said doubtfully.

'It has to happen some time.'

Katrina stared at Sam, who was watching the brightly coloured butterfly mobile dangling over her head.

The thought of being separated from her baby for even a short time made her feel uncomfortable. Yet the last thing she wanted was turn into one of those over-protective mothers.

'It wouldn't be for very long,' Alex encouraged softly. 'Just a couple of hours to start with.'

'I know.' Her mouth twisted. 'I'm being silly.'

Alex shook his head. 'No, you're not. You're just being protective, which is what every mother should be. Never apologise for that. Never.'

He spoke so fervently that Katrina knew he had to be talking from personal experience. She wanted to ask what had happened to make him feel that way, but wasn't sure how to frame the question hovering on the tip of her tongue.

In the end she swallowed the words back. There was more than one way to skin a cat. She could ask the same question in a roundabout way. 'I don't like the idea of leaving Sam with strangers. Maybe your mother could look after her?'

Even before she'd finished speaking, Alex was shaking his head. 'I don't think so.'

'Why not? I'd much rather have her minded by a relative. I'd have thought you'd prefer that too.'

'In some instances relatives can be worse than strangers,' Alex said roughly.

'Oh.'

A void opened up inside her, filled with cold and whistling winds.

'Just what kind of family did he come from?' It was only when she saw the way Alex was staring at her that Katrina realised she'd asked the question out loud.

'Let's just say that being strong and protective weren't my mother's strong points,' Alex said in the same grim voice. 'When I was a kid I could have done with someone like you fighting in my corner. I admire you for the way you've fought for Sam every step of the way.'

A wedge of emotion formed in the back of her throat. It wasn't so much what Alex had said that made her feel sad but what he hadn't said. Instinct warned her that when he'd described his childhood as being lousy it had been an understatement.

'You haven't told your family about Sam, have you?' she asked quietly.

Alex couldn't hide his surprise. 'How did you know that?'

She shrugged. 'It was a simple matter of deduction. If you'd told your mother, she'd have been around here in a flash. After all, I'm presuming Sam is her first grandchild?'

'Yes, she is.'

Katrina squeezed her hands tightly together in front of her. 'Why didn't you tell them?'

She could tell from the look on Alex's face that this was a conversation he would prefer to avoid. 'As you've no doubt gathered, we're not close. What you don't know is that my family is actually a disaster.'

The look in his eyes chilled her to the bone. Her scalp contracted. Her stomach shrunk to the size of a pea.

Alex raked a hand through his hair and towards the back of his neck, got halfway through then stopped the action abruptly. 'I'll tell you the bare bones and then I don't want to talk about it again. OK?'

'OK.'

Her stomach shrunk some more until it felt in danger of disappearing altogether.

'My father was abusive.'

The world stilled and then tilted in on its axis. Her heart hammered.

'What…what do you mean by "abusive"?' She could hardly get the word out. Even the taste of it on her tongue was obscene.

His eyes didn't waver from hers. 'I won't go into details. Suffice to say that my brother and I were mistreated both emotionally and physically by him.'

Katrina gasped; she couldn't help it. Her hand crept protectively to the base of her throat. 'That's awful.'

She didn't think Alex even heard her. He barked out a harsh laugh that had no amusement in it. 'He always claimed that he hurt us for our own good, so that we'd grow up to be good and strong. You know? Character building. It was a lie, of course. He was just a sick bully who got what he deserved in the end.'

The hand at her throat inched higher. When he'd mentioned being bullied she'd never imagined that it had been at the hands of his own father. 'What…what happened to him?'

The eyes that met hers were as cold as chips of blue ice. 'I put him behind bars where he belongs.'

'He's in prison?'

Alex nodded. 'He received a thirty-five-year sentence. Frankly, I hope he never gets out.'

A shiver made its way up and down her spine. 'I'm sorry, Alex. I can't imagine what you must have gone through.'

'It was a long time ago,' he said dismissively. 'I kept hoping my mother would stop him, but she didn't.'

An invisible hand reached into her chest and twisted—hard. 'She was probably too scared.'

'That's what she said. One of the charities I sponsor is for the victims of domestic violence. I've heard a lot of stories over the years, so I know how easy it is for these situations to escalate. Mum was in an impossible position. I know that—with my head. But in my heart I've always found it difficult to forgive her.'

'I can understand that,' Katrina said softly. 'But not everyone is as strong as you. I'm sure she did her best in her own way.'

'Maybe.' His answer was clearly noncommittal.

'And your brother…?'

If she'd thought his expression had been grim until now, it was nothing to the bleakness that etched into every line of his face when she asked that question. 'I tried to protect him as best I could but it wasn't enough.'

Once again it was what Alex had left out that was revealing. No doubt by trying to protect his brother Alex had had to endure more himself.

'Michael couldn't cope,' Alex continued. 'He found his escape in drugs.'

Her heart contracted. 'Oh no. That's so sad.'

She remembered back to the conversation between Alex and Dr Kershew that day in his surgery. The doctor had told Alex that if there was anything he could do to help all he had to do was call. And Alex had replied that the first step was up to Michael. No doubt Michael Webber's drug addiction was what they'd been talking about.

'You've tried to help him, haven't you?' she asked.

Alex raked a hand through his hair and around the back of his neck again. He seemed to have aged during their conversation. 'Of course I've tried. He's my little brother. But Michael hates rehab and always refuses to go. Twice I've virtually kidnapped him when he's either been passed out or so high he didn't know what was going on around him. I've admitted him to the private clinic, but each time he's simply walked out.'

Katrina placed a hand on his arm. 'I'm sorry. That must be difficult for you.'

'It is.' He sounded weary. 'Every time I see him, I try and persuade him to get help, but he never listens.'

'Maybe he's just scared.'

'Maybe.' Alex splayed his hands wide and gave her a twisted smile that held not an ounce of humour. 'So, there you have it—the Webber family, warts and all.'

Katrina was silent for a long moment. It was difficult to know what to say that wasn't trivial or meaning-less. 'Well, I can understand why you wouldn't want your mother looking after Sam, but I'd still like to meet her one day. And your brother.'

'One day.'

Katrina sighed. His response suggested that it wouldn't be any time soon. 'Which brings us back to childcare for Sam.'

He looked relieved that she'd changed the subject.

'Yes. Like you, I want to make sure Sam is looked after properly. I don't want to risk anything happening to her.' The acidic tone of his voice made it clear he was thinking of his childhood and what had happened to him. 'Which rules out babysitters. I don't want a parade of different people coming and going.'

'So, what do you suggest? It sounds to me as though we've ruled out just about everything.'

'Not quite.' Alex smiled in an obvious attempt to shake off the serious mood that had settled over them. 'I was thinking about a part-time nanny. Someone who is available for a set number of hours per week but flexible about when they'll be required. If we offer a generous salary, we should attract some excellent candidates.'

Katrina nodded thoughtfully. 'It sounds like our best bet. But I suspect it won't be easy to find the right person.'

'I know. We're both going to be picky. But there has to be someone out there who we'll be happy with.'

Katrina shrugged. 'Well, we won't know until we try, I suppose.'

'So, there you have it.' He gave her a pointed look. 'With that lot, you'll be too busy to think about going back to work.'

Katrina's smile dimmed a little. 'I don't know about that. They're all projects that won't last more than a month or two.'

'By then there will be other things, like decorating the new house.'

'Don't push, Alex. I've already said I'll think about it. OK?'

'OK.' His eyes glinted. 'Now, there's just the little matter of payment to take care of.' He held out his hand. 'Come here, woman.'

Katrina waved her hand at their half-empty plates. 'What about breakfast?'

Alex snagged her hand and pulled her towards him. 'Forget the food. I have another appetite that needs feeding.'

CHAPTER NINE

ON MONDAY morning Alex was getting dressed in the bedroom Katrina now shared with him when he heard her murmur, 'Good morning,' behind him.

He looked up and smiled then moved to the side of the bed. 'Good morning. Did you sleep well?'

She nodded. 'I did.'

'So did I. No doubt it's all that fresh air we got yesterday,' he said, referring to their trip to Centennial Park to feed the ducks. It was their daughter's first experience with the real variety, rather than the plastic version which shared her bathtime.

Alex leaned down and pressed a drugging kiss against her mouth. By the time he lifted his head they were both breathing heavily. 'If I didn't have an important meeting this morning, I'd join you. But unfortunately I can't.'

Katrina stretched, arching her back and then, in a movement Alex was sure was accidentally-on-purpose, let the sheet fall to her waist.

Alex threw back his head and laughed. 'Witch.' Then he reached down and cupped her breast, fingering the tip until it contracted into a hardened peak.

Katrina groaned in the back of her throat.

Why that sound should send his blood pressure sky-rocketing, Alex wasn't sure, but it did.

'Maybe I can be a little late,' he said huskily, rapidly undoing his tie and pulling it free from the collar, his shirt following. 'Or maybe a lot,' he groaned as he came down on the bed beside her. 'I have the feeling I'm going to be very, *very* late.'

What followed blew his mind. He reached a peak he didn't think it was possible to reach, so dizzyingly high that he felt lightheaded.

'Was there anyone else while you were away?' he demanded. He hadn't planned on asking the question, but suddenly he needed to know.

She pulled away from him just far enough to look into his face. 'You mean a man?'

He nodded.

He already knew that Peter Strauss, Katrina's erstwhile landlord, wasn't a threat. The Royce Agency had furnished him with a report that indicated the man was on a six-month assignment interstate and had merely rented the apartment to Katrina at minimal rent rather than leave it vacant.

Katrina herself had let slip that Strauss was the brother of the friend she'd stayed with when she'd first disappeared.

But that didn't mean that there hadn't been somebody else.

'You have to be kidding! I felt sick for the first four months, and by then I was big and getting bigger every day. And besides…'

'Besides what?' he asked when she failed to continue.

She angled her chin. 'Besides, at the time I was still under the misapprehension that I loved you.'

Alex felt an emotion he didn't want to examine too closely twist his heart tight.

Katrina moved away and pulled the sheet up to her chin. 'But you can't say the same, can you? I saw the pictures in the paper.'

Her voice was flat, the look in her eyes even flatter.

Alex felt tension string his flesh tightly together. 'No. No, I can't.'

'Just how many women did you *enjoy yourself* with while I was away giving birth to your daughter?' she asked with the same kind of sting a bee would be proud of.

'There weren't as many as you think,' he said quietly.

There had been women, sure. But he'd soon realised that sleeping with them was a waste of time.

They hadn't satisfied him the way Katrina had.

They hadn't made his senses reach for the stars.

They hadn't made his heart— His heart what…?

His heart had nothing to do with this, Alex assured himself.

It was just sex. Fantastic sex, admittedly; so fantastic that it was difficult to compete with.

But apart from their daughter that was all there was between them.

The days and weeks rolled into one.

Katrina was run off her feet. She'd found a couple of houses that had potential, but she was determined to wait until she found one that met all of their requirements before showing Alex.

They had time. Although Samantha was growing at

a rate of knots, she wouldn't be walking for several months yet.

She'd also compiled a dossier on two schools she thought would be good for Samantha. After getting Alex's seal of approval, she'd sent letters off to both, requesting a full information-pack complete with application form.

The nanny issue had sorted itself out quite by accident. It turned out that Leslie, their current part-time housekeeper, wanted more hours, and after some discussion Katrina had offered her a live-in position as housekeeper-nanny.

On the home front things were pretty much wonder-ful. She and Alex were growing closer with every day that passed.

One day Alex came home from work with a huge, white glossy box tied with a gold ribbon. 'This is for you,' he said, handing it to her.

Katrina took it automatically. 'What is it?'

'Why don't you open it and find out?'

She placed the box on the glass-topped coffee table and carefully undid the bow. Removing the lid, she folded back the gold tissue-paper sitting on top.

She glanced at Alex when she was presented with black satin. Gently she picked it up. It was a short nightgown, trimmed with lace. One look told her that it was expensive.

'Every woman deserves beautiful nightwear,' Alex said huskily, gesturing between the garment and the box.

It was then Katrina noticed there was something else in the box. In fact there were several somethings—two more nightgowns, one in the most gorgeous ivory colour, and the other a pale lilac.

A lump formed in the back of her throat. 'I don't know what to say. I've never owned anything so beautiful.'

'"Thank you" might be a good place to start,' Alex said, and held out his arms.

Katrina rose to her feet and went into his embrace eagerly, rose onto the balls of her feet and offered him her mouth.

When he finally lifted his head they were both breathing heavily. 'I think we should retire to our bedroom and you can parade them for me.'

The glint of his eyes told her that he would do more than just look. Holding hands, they began walking down the corridor. 'I guess I can throw out my old trackie and T-shirt I usually sleep in,' Katrina said.

Alex came to an abrupt halt. 'No! Don't do that.'

Katrina turned to face him and was surprised to see colour striping his sculptured cheekbones. 'Why not?'

He gave her a rueful smile. 'I happen to think you look sexy as all hell in them.'

'You do?' She couldn't hide her surprise.

'I do.'

'Then why the nightgowns?'

'They're more for you than for me. I just wanted you to have something nice.'

Another lump formed in the back of her throat. It was a lovely gesture, and proved how thoughtful Alex could be.

There was just one thing wrong with that: she'd wanted to keep emotionally detached. But her reaction indicated it was too late for that.

* * *

One night Katrina woke to find she was alone in bed. With a frown, she was about to get up and investigate when she heard Alex's voice on the baby monitor.

Realising he was in the nursery, she subsided back against the pillow, listening curiously.

'Hello, Princess. What are you doing awake at this time of night? You should be asleep,' he said softly.

An indecipherable gurgle, barely loud enough for Katrina to hear, was his response.

She heard a rustling noise; it sounded as if Alex had picked Samantha up out of her cot.

'So you can't sleep either, huh? Neither can I. Maybe we should keep each other company for a while.'

The baby cooed, as if to say that it was a good idea.

'What woke you up, I wonder?' Alex said, keeping his voice low. 'You can't be hungry. You drank as much milk as a baby brontosaurus.' There was a pause, then, 'What did you say? Not as much as a brontosaurus, huh? OK. What about a tyrannosaurus rex? You're happy with that? Good.'

Katrina smiled.

In this mood, Alex could charm the bees from the trees.

'OK. That's settled—you're not awake because you're hungry. So what does that leave us with, Princess?' Alex murmured. 'Maybe you had a bad dream, like your daddy did? Is that it?'

The baby cooed.

Katrina, who was still listening, felt her smile slip a little.

'No. You look and sound far too happy to have had a nightmare. I bet I know what it is—you knew your daddy was having bad dreams so you woke up just so you could make me feel better.'

A wedge of emotion formed in the back of Katrina's throat.

'And do you know what? It's worked. How can I stay sad about those nasty things in my dreams when I have you around, huh?'

There was silence for a while.

Katrina knew she was eavesdropping on what was a private conversation—even if it was only one way—but she couldn't stop listening now. She waited with bated breath to hear what he said next.

She didn't have long to wait.

'Do you know something else? My father told me that when I had brats of my own I'd understand what he did to us. But he was wrong; I don't understand. I'll never understand. And you're not a brat. You're my princess.'

The wedge of emotion in Katrina's throat expanded until she could barely breathe.

She'd often woken in the middle of the night to find Alex not in their bed. She'd mentioned his restlessness to him several times, and Alex had admitted to the occasional nightmare about his childhood, but hadn't really wanted to discuss it. She'd always wondered what the nightmares had been about.

Now she knew.

With a shaky hand, she reached out and turned the monitor off.

She couldn't listen any more.

When Alex came in some time later, Katrina pretended to be asleep. She almost gave herself away when he pulled her into his arms, but she simply snuggled into him.

As she fell asleep in her lover's arms Katrina realised there was one positive to come out of what she'd heard—and that was that father and daughter were growing closer.

Despite the way everything was progressing so smoothly, Katrina wasn't entirely happy. She was aware of a low-grade discontent hovering just beneath the surface, like a toothache that just wouldn't go away.

This feeling came to a head on one particularly sunny Sunday when they put Samantha in her pram and drove to Bondi beach.

They were strolling along the promenade when it happened.

Because the weather was so nice, lots of other people were doing the same thing. Katrina found herself watching the other couples they passed.

No doubt she and Alex looked the same. No doubt with Samantha in her pram they looked just like all the other families.

But something was missing.

And that was when it hit her: somehow she'd fallen in love with Alex all over again.

She wasn't quite sure when it had happened. It wasn't as though it had hit her like a bolt of lightning. There had been no cymbals and drums, no choir of angels.

It had been a gradual thing that had crept up on her. It was there inside her, like a living thing.

She wanted to be like those other couples—in love, and loved in return.

But that was an impossibility, wasn't it?

What chance did she have of Alex falling in love with her when he didn't even believe in the emotion?

Alex liked and respected her. He was committed to her and their daughter. Surely that meant that he cared for her in his own way?

The more she thought about it, the more she was convinced that she was right.

Alex must feel something for her.

Otherwise how could he look at her with tenderness in his eyes? And how could he make love to her as if she was the most precious thing on earth?

Feeling marginally better, Katrina turned her attention to something else that had been bothering her.

It had niggled at the back of her mind for the last week but she couldn't quite put her finger on what was wrong.

Whatever it was, it was as elusive as the wind and as indefinable as the clouds rolling across the sky.

Katrina watched as another couple strolled towards them. The woman was pushing a pram; the man had a little boy of three or four sitting on his shoulders.

The little boy said something and tugged on his father's hair. The man laughed and reached a hand above his head, scooped the child into his arms and began tickling him.

Katrina stopped walking and stared.

There was something in the picture she was looking at that epitomised what it was that was bothering her. Still, she couldn't pin down exactly what it was.

Frustration imploded inside her. It was like a word sitting on the tip of your tongue that you just couldn't quite spit out.

She was sure that if she looked hard enough the answer would come to her, but it didn't.

'What is it?' Alex asked beside her.

Katrina gave herself a mental shake and forced a smile to her stiff lips. Whatever it was, it would come to her in its own good time. 'Nothing.'

Samantha chose that moment to start crying, saving Katrina from any further explanation, something she was thankful for.

Because, although she hadn't been able to figure out exactly what it was that was bothering her, she *had* drawn one conclusion. Whatever it was, it had something to do with Alex and Samantha's relationship.

And whatever it was it wasn't good.

Later that night Katrina woke to find she was alone in bed.

She made no move to get up and investigate. She was getting used to Alex's middle-of-the-night wanderings. No doubt another nightmare had woken him.

Sometimes he would go in to the nursery but as often as not Samantha was asleep and he would tiptoe out as quietly as he'd gone in.

Katrina was never able to go back to sleep during these times. Instead she lay there worrying about Alex—which was exactly what she was doing now.

Suddenly, she heard Alex's voice on the baby monitor.

'Hello, Princess. So you're awake tonight, are you?'

The baby let out a cry, barely loud enough for Katrina to hear.

She heard the familiar rustling sound of Alex picking Samantha up out of her cot.

'You're as pretty as your mother. Do you know that?'

Katrina's throat clogged with emotion.

Maybe he did care for her just a little bit. Maybe there *was* a chance he'd fall in love with her.

She heard Alex mutter something, but she couldn't make out what it was. She then heard a couple of sounds she couldn't decipher.

The next thing she knew, the bedroom door was flung back on its hinges. She jumped a foot in the air. 'What the…?' she gasped, bolting upright, her hand pressing against her chest. 'You scared me half to death!'

'Sorry.' He paused for a heartbeat then said in a voice she barely recognised, 'Sam's sick. We need to take her to the hospital.'

For the first time Katrina noticed that their daughter was cradled in his arms.

She blinked rapidly.

Her brain felt as if it was encased in fog, yet at the same time it was as clear as it had ever been.

Because suddenly what had been bothering her just smacked her across the face. Alex was never as relaxed with his daughter as the man at the beach had been with his son.

It was a subtle thing, which explained why it had been so difficult to pin down. But it was there.

He was never entirely at ease with her. It wasn't that he was tense, exactly, but he was never completely comfortable either.

Why?

Although she desperately wanted an answer to that question, now was not the time.

What Alex had just said cut through her thoughts like

the blade of a knife cutting through butter. 'What's wrong with her? Are you sure it's not just that she's teething?'

'No, it's more than that. I'll tell you as you get dressed. But we need to get moving. Now!'

The urgency in his voice spun Katrina into immediate action. She threw back the covers, hurried to the wardrobe and grabbed the first article of clothing that came to hand.

'Tell me,' she ordered as she pulled on her jeans.

'She has a fever. Her skin is blotchy. And she's not focussing properly.'

The list of symptoms made her freeze before she started to shake so hard she thought she might fall into a million pieces. 'What…what do you think is wrong with her?'

Alex shook his head, face grim. 'I don't know. But we need to get to the hospital as soon as possible.'

What followed was a nightmare.

They went immediately to the emergency department. As soon as they were inside, Alex said, 'We need a doctor. Right now!'

He possessed such an air of authority that a nurse immediately snapped to attention. After the briefest of examinations, she took Samantha and hurried out of the waiting area into the main emergency-room.

Alex and Katrina followed through the swing doors and watched as the nurse handed her charge over to a female doctor in her mid-forties. The conversation was brief. Although they were too far away to hear what was being said, their body language and the sense of urgency that surrounded them suggested the initial prognosis was not good.

A shaft of fear speared through Katrina's heart.

'You can't come in here,' the nurse said, spying them a moment later. 'You'll have to stay in the waiting room.'

Alex took Katrina's hand in his and squeezed it tight. The look he threw the nurse made her blink. 'We're not leaving.'

'But, sir—'

'We're staying here.' His tone brooked no argument; his face was hard and determined.

Alex and Katrina continued to hover in the background as Samantha was hooked up to an IV drip, and what appeared to be samples of blood were taken.

The longer they worked on her, the greater Katrina's fear became. 'If anything happens to Sam…' she muttered.

Alex wrapped an arm around her waist. 'Sam is going to be fine. The doctors know what they're doing.'

Katrina certainly hoped so.

Each minute ticked by with mind-numbing slowness. Neither she nor Alex moved an inch, nor did they speak. Katrina wasn't even sure they were breathing.

Eventually the female doctor hurried over to them. 'I'm Dr Niven. You are the child's parents?'

'We are.' It was Alex who replied, voice tense.

'What's her name?'

'Samantha. Sam.' Again, it was Alex who replied.

'OK. Well, we suspect Sam has meningitis.'

The word gouged at Katrina like hungry teeth until she felt as though she were bleeding inside. A moan escaped her strangled throat and her knees collapsed beneath her. If Alex hadn't been holding her, she would have fallen to the floor.

'Are you sure?' Alex asked, his voice reed-thin.

Dr Niven shook her head. 'No, we're not. We've put her on antibiotics just in case. And we've taken a sample of her spinal fluid for testing. We're going to rush the results through. We should know for certain in a couple of hours.'

'And if it *is* meningitis?' Alex asked.

Katrina's heart leapt into her throat. She knew what he was asking and wasn't sure she wanted to hear the answer.

'Then we'll continue with the antibiotics and monitor her progress. There's nothing more we can do.'

There's nothing more we can do.

Why did those words have a ring of finality to them?

Katrina swayed but didn't fall, Alex still holding her up.

'There has to be something I can do.' Alex was unable to hide his desperation. 'I can pay for the best specialist there is. Just tell me their name and I'll fly them in.'

'I'm sure you can. But it's not necessary. If it's meningitis, the best treatment is antibiotics.' The doctor patted his arm. 'That and lots of love, of course.'

Alex nodded then half-urged, half-carried Katrina across to Samantha's bed. He gently deposited her in a dull grey visitor's chair. Katrina felt like a rag doll with no power of her own to function.

She was aware of Alex pulling up a chair beside her but she didn't look at him; her entire focus was on their baby daughter.

Willing her to live.

Willing her to get better.

Alex stared at Samantha.

She looked lost in the adult-sized hospital bed with her little arm hooked up to the IV-drip.

They'd been waiting for what seemed like hours. A nurse came and went at regular intervals to check Samantha's temperature, blood pressure and whatever else the monitor she was attached to registered.

Every time he asked the same question: 'How is she?'

And every time the answer was the same: 'There's no change.'

Alex balled his hands into fists, his heart slamming against his ribcage. She looked so tiny and vulnerable. So young and defenceless.

A hollow formed in the pit of his stomach until it felt like a never-ending ravine filled with cold, whistling winds. Alex felt it pulling at him as if it was trying to suck the life out of him.

If Samantha died, Alex feared he'd disappear into the abyss for ever.

He couldn't lose Samantha. He couldn't let her die.

Fear beat on the inside of his skull with the force of a jackhammer.

Anxiety squeezed his heart with razor-sharp talons until he thought it might burst.

He wanted to jump to his feet and scream with rage. He wanted to howl at the gods for doing this to him.

He turned to Katrina. She looked shattered. Her face was pale and pinched, hands clenched so tightly together that her knuckles had turned white.

He placed a hand over her firmly woven fists. 'She'll be OK,' he said, imbuing his voice with a confidence he was far from feeling inside.

'If something happens to her…'

'*Nothing* is going to happen to her.' His eyes returned to Samantha who looked smaller and more fragile every time he looked at her. 'She's going to be OK. She *has* to be OK.'

Katrina was silent for a long moment and then she said quietly, 'You love her, don't you?'

His gut tightened. A lump the size and weight of a small bus formed in the back of his throat. 'Yes, I love her.'

It was there with every beat of his heart and every breath that he breathed.

Katrina turned her hands over and squeezed his tight.

Despite the gravity of the situation the corners of his mouth lifted. 'Aren't you going to say "I told you so"?'

She shook her head. 'No. I'm just glad…for both your sakes.'

So was Alex.

But as he looked at his gravely ill daughter Alex realised that he owed her some recompense.

He was a thief. A thief who had robbed Samantha of his heart. He'd spent time with her, done all the right things, but he'd been holding a part of himself back.

If Samantha died he would regret every minute he'd chosen not to give all of himself to her.

She had to live.

CHAPTER TEN

Six hours later they were still sitting there.

Still waiting.

Alex had never felt so helpless. Tension compressed his spine until it felt half its normal length.

Katrina sat as still as a statue beside him.

Alex did the exact opposite. He sat forwards. Then backwards. Then forwards again. Rested his head in his hands. Raked his hands through his hair and around the back of his neck.

Finally, he'd had enough.

He jumped to his feet, hands clenched tightly at his sides. 'I can't stand this! I have to find out what's going on.'

Katrina didn't answer him. She didn't look capable of it.

The look on her face gutted him. Swallowing hard, Alex gave her shoulder a reassuring squeeze before striding to the nurses' station, where he demanded to see the doctor.

'I want answers!' he said, when Dr Niven finally appeared.

The look she gave him was measured and calm. 'I know you do. So do I. But we have to wait while pathology runs the tests. It shouldn't be too long now.'

Alex shoved his hands deep into his pockets. He knew he was being unreasonable but he couldn't help it. 'I just—'

The doctor placed a hand on his arm. 'I know. You don't have to explain.'

'Alex…?'

The voice came from behind him.

Alex spun on his heel. He blinked. Then blinked again. He couldn't believe what he was seeing.

Because standing in front of him were his mother and brother.

'Mum. Michael. What on earth are you doing here?'

Audrey Webber raised a brow, hands folded in front of her thickened waistline. 'We're here to support you, of course.'

'I don't understand.' Alex shook his head, as if the action could clear his confusion. 'How did you even know I was here?'

This time it was Michael who answered. 'It was on the news. They said your daughter had been admitted to hospital. Is it true? Do you have a daughter?'

Alex nodded. Someone must have recognised him and leaked the story to the press.

What a terrible way for his family to have found out. He opened his mouth to apologise but his mother got in first.

'Why didn't you tell us?' She held up a hand. 'No, don't answer that. It's not important right now. How is she?'

'She's—'

'Alex.'

This time it was Katrina's voice saying his name. Alex froze. For a heartbeat he didn't move. Then he spun towards the doorway.

'What's happened?' He had to force the words past the constriction in his throat. 'Is she worse?' he asked, not at all sure he wanted to know the answer.

Even before she spoke Alex noticed Katrina's shaky smile. 'Sam's started to respond to the treatment. The doctor is with her now.'

The relief was so powerful that his insides sagged. 'Thank God for that!' He turned to his mother and brother. 'I have to go, but I'll be back as soon as I can.'

Audrey pointed to the row of grey visitors' chairs similar to the ones he and Katrina had been sitting on for so many hours. 'You go and do what you have to do. Michael and I will wait here.'

Emotion rose up inside him like a tidal wave. Sweeping an arm around each of them he pulled them close. 'Thank you,' he said in a choked voice. 'It means a lot to me that you're here.'

He meant every word. His mother's support in particular went straight to his heart, and he found himself blinking back tears as he strode to Katrina's side.

He held her hand tightly as they approached the doctor.

'The diagnosis of meningitis has been confirmed,' Dr Niven said. 'That's the bad news. The good news is that the antibiotics have started to do their job. Sam's vital signs are improving.'

'How long before she's out of danger?' Alex asked. Although Samantha's response to the antibiotics was fantastic news, he didn't want to count his blessings too soon.

'Another twelve hours should do it.'

Alex nodded.

'I notice you have other family who have arrived. Please keep the visitors to two at a time.' The doctor placed a hand on Alex's arm. 'You saved your daughter's life with your quick action. It would have been too late if you'd left it to morning,' she said before departing.

'Oh, Alex,' Katrina said 'If you hadn't…'

He didn't want Katrina thinking about what might have happened. He didn't want to go there himself.

'But I did,' he reassured her quickly.

And he always would.

The thought, which had ridden immediately on the back of the first, almost knocked the legs out from under him.

He felt as if he'd driven smack-bang into a brick wall at high speed. 'Shattered' would be an understatement.

He reeled backwards.

Katrina caught his arm and guided him towards a seat. 'Alex! What is it?'

For a minute, he couldn't speak. He couldn't even breathe. The sound of his blood pounding at his temples was deafening.

'Should I get the doctor?' Katrina asked worriedly beside him.

'No.' He grabbed her arm. 'Just give me a minute.'

She nodded and held his hand.

He dragged in a breath. Then another. And slowly his heartbeat returned to normal.

He flung himself against the rigid back of the chair. 'God, I've been such a fool!'

Katrina shook her head, green eyes clearly confused. 'I don't understand.'

'I know you don't.' He looked at the bed then back at Katrina. 'I was petrified I was going to hurt her.'

She gasped, her body jerking against his side. Her eyes narrowed on his face. 'What on earth are you talking about?'

'My father's blood runs through my veins. Something made him into a monster. I kept on thinking: what's to say the same thing can't happen to me?'

Katrina shook her head vehemently, her grip on his hand so tight her nails dug in to his flesh. 'It wouldn't happen.'

'I know that now. But for a long time I thought it could.'

Her eyes flashed. 'Is that why you had the vasectomy?'

Alex nodded. 'My father was always telling me how much alike we were. Taunting me with it. And it's true; we're similar in lots of ways. I grew up believing that I'd turn out just like him.'

'That's abuse in its own right,' Katrina said thoughtfully. 'But, still, a vasectomy was a rather drastic measure to take when there was absolutely no evidence to support your theory,' she said with a frown.

His gut twisted tight. And then again, even tighter. 'There was evidence. Or, at least, I thought there was.'

'Tell me.'

Alex ran a hand over his face. 'Back then I was full of rage over what my father was doing to us. One day at school, my best friend said something I didn't like. To this day, I can't even remember what it was. I punched him in the face—so hard that I broke his nose.'

'Oh, Alex,' she said, her voice drenched with sadness.

Alex didn't want her sympathy. But he did want her understanding. 'But do you know what the worst thing was?'

She shook her head.

'The worst thing was that on one level I enjoyed it. Oh, I was sorry that I'd hurt Jason, because we were mates and he was one of the few people who made my life bearable. But on another level it felt good—hitting him got rid of some of the pent-up anger. And suddenly I saw my father's face when he hit me and I wondered whether I had the same look on my face when I hit Jason. And I thought: it's *really* happening. I'm turning out exactly like my father. That was the day I decided to have the vasectomy. It seemed to be the only way to break the cycle.'

'And that's why you've been holding a part of your-self back with Sam during the last month,' Katrina murmured as if she were speaking to herself.

Alex frowned. 'I admit I've been cautious. And now you can understand why. But I didn't think it was noticeable.'

'It wasn't entirely. I sensed something wasn't quite right, but I couldn't figure out what it was. Until tonight.'

He raised an eyebrow.

'When you carried Sam into our bedroom I suddenly realised you were never entirely at ease with her. Not the way you should be. After what you've just told me, my guess is that you were being over-cautious.'

Alex frowned again and then shook his head. 'You could be right. I'm a fool.'

He didn't believe in fate. He preferred to believe that a man could shape his own destiny. So why had he been stupid enough to believe that genetics could override his true nature?

'I'm not going to disagree with you,' she said, once again wielding the words as if they were a plank of wood she was hitting around his head.

The corners of his mouth turned up. 'Little Miss Confrontation strikes again, does she?'

'You'd better believe it. I can understand why you might have thought you could turn out like your father in the beginning. You were in an untenable situation. But, later, you should have known there wasn't a chance of it happening.'

'You sound very sure.'

'That's because I am. I know *you*.' She tilted her head to one side. 'Tell me something.'

His eyes narrowed on her face. 'If I can.'

She waited for a moment before asking softly, 'Did you try to take some of your brother's beatings for him?'

Alex gasped. He couldn't help it. 'How did you know that?'

'You mentioned that you'd tried to protect him. I simply guessed the rest.' She raised her eyebrows. 'Do you really think a man who's prepared to do that would ever hurt anyone, let alone a defenceless child?'

Alex shook his head. 'You're a lot wiser than me.'

'No. You've just been a bit too harsh with yourself; I believe that's a common trait of high achievers.' She nodded towards the doorway. 'I think you may have been a bit harsh with your mother, too. What say you introduce us?'

Alex clasped her hand in his and led her out to the

waiting area. On the way he sent up a silent prayer of thanks.

Not just because Samantha was on the mend. But also for giving him Katrina.

Once he'd only seen her beauty, but now he could see her strength and intelligence.

Alex admired her more and more with every day that passed. If he had chosen a mother for his child, he could not have chosen more perfectly.

His two girls.

His two *special* girls.

How could a man get so lucky?

For the next twelve days they kept a constant vigil at Samantha's bedside, taking it in turns to eat, shower and sleep.

On the third day, Alex found himself alone with his mother in the hospital cafeteria, where they had queued to buy coffees to take back upstairs.

That morning Samantha had been pronounced out of danger and at Alex's insistence had been moved into her own private room.

'I meant what I said the other day,' Alex said. 'I really appreciate you being here for me.'

Audrey's eyes—the same eyes that Alex, Michael and Samantha had all inherited—met his. 'Like I wasn't before? Is that what you're saying?'

Alex shifted uncomfortably. 'Mum…'

She laid a hand on his arm. 'It's OK, Alex. I know what you think, and I understand. But just remember that your memories are those of a young, frightened boy, and an angry and just-as-frightened teenager.'

Alex took her arm and led her to an empty table.
Pulling out one of the inevitably grey plastic chairs that
dotted the public areas of the hospital he motioned for
her to sit down.

When they were both seated, he said, 'Tell me.'

Alex wasn't sure why he was prepared to listen to his
mother's version of events after so many years.

Maybe it was because Samantha's illness had reminded him that life was short.

Maybe it was because he'd made such a terrible
mistake when Katrina had told him she was pregnant
and he was prepared to accept he might have made a
similar mistake with his mother.

And maybe it was because realising he was nothing
like his father had somehow had a cathartic effect. It certainly felt as if a void had opened up between him and
the past. The memories were still there, but they
couldn't hurt him any more.

They talked for over an hour. When they finally left
the cafeteria, Alex felt they'd taken the first tentative
steps towards putting the past behind them.

On the eighth day, Alex found himself alone with
Michael at Samantha's bedside.

Just that morning Samantha had given them her first
smile since falling ill. Katrina had cried; Alex had felt
like joining her.

Michael gestured to his niece with a bony hand.
'Why didn't you tell us about her, bro?'

Alex shook his head. 'I'm not sure. I guess I didn't
want to taint her with our past.'

Michael punched him on the arm. 'Hey, aren't you the one who keeps on telling me the past is in the past and that we should leave it there and move on?'

Alex nodded gravely. 'I am. I guess I'm not good at taking my own advice.'

Then, without planning on doing it, Alex found himself admitting to Michael what he had so far only admitted to himself and Katrina—that he had been terrified of turning out like their father.

Michael's reaction was to laugh his head off. When he finally managed to speak, he said, 'You're as screwed up as I am.'

Looking at his brother long and hard, Alex shook his head. 'I'm not any more. What about you?'

They both knew Alex was referring to Michael's drug addiction.

For the first time since the conversation started, Michael looked away. 'It's not that easy, bro.'

'I know it's not. But promise me you'll think about it.'

Michael nodded.

It wasn't a very enthusiastic nod, but it was still the first time Michael had agreed to consider getting help. Although he knew there was still a long way to go, Alex knew this was a hugely positive step forward. He punched his brother on the arm. 'Good man.'

Just then Katrina came in and shooed Michael out.

A feeling of peace settled over Alex. Katrina was his rock. He didn't know how he would have got through this ordeal without her at his side.

In fact, he didn't know what he would do without her, full stop.

On the thirteenth day, Samantha was well enough to go home.

The morning after their return from the hospital, Katrina woke slowly.

It was a pleasant change to have slept in a real bed. For almost two weeks she'd slept in chairs or spare hospital-beds. Once or twice she'd even slept cradled in Alex's arms.

Even before she opened sleep-drenched eyes she was frowning.

Where was Alex?

She knew he wasn't beside her. She didn't need to look; she could feel his absence. They normally slept wrapped in each other's arms—quite literally—legs entangled, her head in the crook of his shoulder. His hands holding her close.

Pulling on her robe, Katrina padded out of the bedroom to investigate.

She found Alex lying on the sofa with Samantha sprawled on his chest. Having recently discovered her own hands, the baby was taking great delight in trying to poke a finger in her father's eye.

Seeing the two of them like this made Katrina's heart melt in her chest.

The barriers between father and daughter had finally come tumbling down.

Alex was no longer hanging back; the distance she'd felt between them no longer existed.

This was what she'd wanted from day one—for Alex to be a father to his daughter.

And what a wonderful father he was. Gentle and caring, and at the same time strong and protective.

There was only one thing that could make life even more perfect. And that was if Alex loved her.

Once she'd thought that was an impossibility. Now there was room for hope.

Alex had claimed not to believe in love, but since then he'd admitted to loving his daughter. Surely that meant there was a chance he could learn to love her too?

Remembering how Alex had acted while they were at the hospital, Katrina was sure there was.

He had been her rock. Supportive. Encouraging. He'd been there to cling to when she'd needed it. And he'd been there to pep her up when she was feeling down.

He obviously cared about her. Wasn't it possible that his feelings could develop into love?

Katrina certainly hoped so.

She was about to tiptoe away when Alex spotted her.

He was relaxed and smiling. 'Good morning.'

Katrina smiled back. 'Good morning.' She gestured to the baby. 'I wondered why it was so quiet.'

Alex grinned. 'Sam woke around six, but you were out for the count so I decided to let you sleep. She's been fed, she's been changed and we've just been playing.'

Katrina smothered a laugh. 'Have you, now?'

'We have. She's very clever, aren't you, Princess?'

Samantha's answer was to smile and gurgle her complete agreement.

'Well, since you have everything under control, I might as well go and have a shower.'

'No. Don't do that.' Alex swung his legs to the floor and sat up. The smile dropped from his face. 'I want to talk to you about something.'

'You sound serious.'

'I am.' He patted the cushion beside him. 'Come and sit down.'

Katrina did as he asked. 'OK. Shoot.'

She wasn't quite sure what she was expecting, but it certainly wasn't what came next.

'I think we should get married.'

Katrina just stared at him.

Her insides stilled at the same time as her heart took off at a gallop.

Licking her lips and dragging in a breath, she said, 'Say that again.'

He didn't hesitate. 'You heard me—I think we ought to get married.'

The breath locked tight in her lungs. She'd heard him right. 'Why?' she asked.

It was the question that stood out amongst all the other thoughts tumbling through her brain.

'Why?' he repeated. He was clearly stunned that she hadn't thrown herself into his arms with an immediate acceptance. 'Isn't marriage the final step in becoming a family? Isn't it a commitment Sam deserves from us?'

His answer felt like a guillotine blade falling from a great height, cutting her heart in two.

She wanted to howl with the pain of it. Alex wanted to marry her because of Samantha, *not* because he loved her.

She pleated the edge of her robe with unsteady fingers, unable and unwilling to look him in the eye for fear he'd see how devastated she was. 'I can't think about that just yet. I can't think about anything. I just want to enjoy having Sam home for a few days.'

He frowned and wrapped an arm around her shoulders. 'I'm sorry. I didn't mean to rush you. I know how stressful the last couple of weeks have been.' He gave her a rather sheepish smile. 'Sam's illness has made me face up to myself. There are a few things I want to do differently from now on, and top of the list is formalising our relationship.'

Katrina suppressed a wince.

There was a huge difference between 'formalising our relationship' and 'I love you'.

The two might as well have been on different planets.

'I understand,' she said, reaching for Samantha.

The problem was that she understood all too well.

Her hopes and dreams lay like dust at her feet.

The big question now was what was she going to do about it?

That night Katrina lay awake for hours.

For a while she just stared at the ceiling. Later, she rolled on her side, propped her head on her raised elbow and watched Alex sleep.

Moonlight streamed in through the windows. It added a silvery sheen to his dark hair and cast shadows on the sculptured lines of his face.

Her heart clenched hard. She kept trying to tell herself that nothing had changed, but it had. It had changed the minute she'd realised she loved Alex. She just hadn't realised it at the time; Samantha's illness had distracted her.

But Alex's proposal had hit her around the face and made her confront the reality of the situation head-on.

Could she stay with Alex—marry him—knowing that she loved him but he didn't love her?

Already the pain of it was eating her up inside. What would years of that do to her?

If she was deeply unhappy, what would that do to Samantha?

Those questions plagued Katrina for the rest of the night. They went around and around in her head until she was dizzy with them.

In the end, she decided it was time to be brave. It was time to be Little Miss Confrontation again and tell Alex how she felt about him.

Yes, she was opening herself up to being hurt again, but it was a risk she had to take. Because only once she knew exactly what Alex felt for her could she decide what to do.

She might just have to sweep the dust of her dreams into the rubbish bin, or she might be able to breathe new life into the dreams themselves.

CHAPTER ELEVEN

ALEX was gone when she woke up. Not just from the bed but from the apartment. She found a note propped next to the kettle telling her he'd decided to let her sleep and that he would try to come home early.

Although his concern was touching, Katrina was disappointed. Now that she'd decided to tell Alex how she felt about him, she could hardly wait to get on with it. But it looked like she had no choice but to wait until he came home.

Mid-morning, Katrina was playing with Samantha on the carpet in the lounge when the phone rang.

She lifted the hands-free receiver to her ear. 'Hello?'

'Could I speak to Alex Webber, please?' an efficient female voice asked.

'I'm afraid he's not here. Can I take a message?'

There was a momentary pause. 'Is that you, Katrina?'

Katrina frowned. She didn't recognise the voice. 'Yes. Who is this?'

'It's Tracey from Dr Kershew's office. How are you? And how is Samantha? We were sorry to hear she'd been in hospital.'

Katrina smiled. 'Yes, it's me, Tracey. I'm fine, and so is Sam. Thank goodness!'

'That's great. Anyway, on to the reason for my call.'

'Certainly. You wanted me to pass on a message to Alex?'

'Yes, please. I was just calling to tell him we've arranged for him to have his vasectomy redone, as he requested. The appointment is scheduled for eleven a.m. on the twenty-eighth of next month at the Royal North Shore Hospital.'

Katrina pressed a hand to her chest.

'Katrina, did you hear me?'

She drew in a deep breath. 'Yes, I heard you; I'm just looking for a piece of paper and a pen so I can write the date down. I'm not sure Alex will be able to make it then.'

By the time she finished with him, he probably wouldn't need the procedure—she might very well take care of it herself with the bluntest instrument she could find!

'If he can't, that's OK. Just get back to me and I'll change the appointment.'

'Fine.'

Katrina didn't say any more. She couldn't. She pressed the button to end the call before the phone dropped from her nerveless fingers.

A vasectomy. She couldn't believe it.

Jumping to her feet, she scooped up her daughter and began to pace, her mind spinning. Thoughts tumbled one over the other like a piece of paper caught in a force-ten gale.

She'd decided to tell Alex that she loved him, but what was the point now?

The answer came back with soul-stripping speed: there was none. She'd told Alex she wanted more children. If he'd been even the teeniest, tiniest bit in love with her, then he wouldn't have arranged to have his vasectomy redone.

The question now was, could she stay?

She felt as if her heart had been ripped to shreds and then dunked in a vat of acid. Years of feeling like that would be intolerable. But what was the alternative? If she didn't stay it meant taking Samantha away from her father.

The bond between father and daughter was as strong as between mother and daughter.

Samantha would miss Alex.

And Alex…

She put trembling fingers to her lips. Alex might not have fallen in love with her but he *had* fallen in love with his daughter. Separating them now would be cruel.

Katrina sank down on the carpet as if the weight of the world was on her shoulders.

How long she remained there, she didn't know.

It could have been minutes or it could have been hours. Her mind was so numb that time didn't seem to have meaning any more.

It was only when Samantha began to cry that she finally moved. Choking back a sob, Katrina raced through to the bedroom. Placing Samantha carefully in the middle of the king-sized bed, she put two pillows on either side of her so the baby couldn't roll off, then went into her old bedroom and pulled her suitcase out of the closet.

Blinking back tears, she returned to the master bedroom and began flinging her clothes willy-nilly into the open suitcase.

The future seemed untenable.

She'd told Alex once that she wasn't good mistress-material. It appeared she wasn't good unloved-wife material either.

Alex frowned as he closed the front door behind him.

The apartment felt different. How, he wasn't quite sure, but it did.

Maybe it was because Katrina wasn't in the lounge as she usually was when he came home.

'Katrina?' he called.

There was no answer. His voice seemed to echo off the walls. A frisson of unease slid down his spine.

A quick search of the apartment showed no sign of either Katrina or Samantha.

They could, of course, have gone for a walk. But somehow Alex didn't think so.

Gut instinct warned him that something else was going on here.

He went back to the bedroom. This time he looked more closely. The frisson of unease settled uncomfortably at the base of his spine and remained there, pricking at him.

The clothes he'd bought Katrina were hanging in the closet, but her toiletries and her own clothes were missing.

He hurried through to the nursery.

Here the difference was even more noticeable. Nappies, wipes, powder—all gone.

But it was the absence of Samantha's pink teddy bear that was the real clincher. Samantha loved that bear; it slept beside her every night.

Alex sank down on a chair.

Only then did he notice the envelope sitting on top of the chest of drawers with his name on it.

He jumped to his feet and tore it open.

The envelope contained a single sheet of paper covered with Katrina's neat hand writing.

Dear Alex,

I'm sorry to spring this on you, but I knew if I told you face to face you'd try and talk me out of it or insist that I leave Sam with you. You've commented several times about how much Sam's illness has changed things for you. Well, it's changed things for me too. Although we're both agreed that giving Sam a proper family is the right thing to do, I just don't know whether I can do it. You said you weren't prepared to sign up for a life of celibacy. Well, I'm not sure I can sign up for a loveless marriage. Please don't worry about Sam. I will take good care of her. I will be in contact soon.

Katrina.

Alex crumpled the note in his clenched fist.

They'd gone. Disappeared. Katrina had packed up their belongings and left. His heart started pounding until he could feel the blood pumping at his temples.

The smell of baby powder lingering in the room seemed to mock him. So too did the yellow rubber-duck that Alex was now such an expert at making quacking noises for.

Where had they gone?

And how on earth was he going to find her?

He'd told Royce to cancel the man tailing Katrina weeks ago. It hadn't seemed necessary any more.

He hoped it wasn't a decision he was going to live to regret.

Katrina had disappeared once before. He remembered her telling him that she wasn't a fan of credit cards; it was her use of cash that had made it so difficult to track her down last time.

If she did the same this time…

Pulling out his mobile phone, he called the agency and filled Royce in. 'I don't care how much it costs. Find them.'

As he hung up, his insides turned to ice. Ice that seemed to saturate every particle of his being until it felt as though he'd never be warm again.

Fear sliced through him until it felt as if he was being skinned alive.

One thought ran through his head, clearer than any other, chilling him to the bone.

What if he never found them?

Two days later Alex was in the middle of his monthly board meeting. He was trying and failing to concentrate on the various presentations.

All he could think about was Katrina and Samantha—and the action he'd taken overnight to flush them out of wherever it was they were hiding.

Suddenly, the double doors to the boardroom were thrown forcefully open. The handles hit the wall with a crash, the sound so loud he stopped speaking mid sentence.

All eyes, including his, turned in that direction.

Katrina was standing in the open doorway, caramel hair swirling around her shoulders.

She looked magnificent.

She also looked angry.

Her cat-like green eyes were spitting emerald fire, fury striping her razor-sharp cheekbones a bright, burning red. Alex suspected one look would be enough to set the long boardroom table on fire.

'Out!' she instructed, her eyes never leaving Alex's face.

The board looked in his direction for guidance. From the look on their faces, they clearly expected him to tell Katrina to wait outside until the meeting was over. They knew he allowed nothing to interfere with these monthly gatherings.

What they didn't realise was that the Webber Investment Bank was no longer the most important thing in Alex's life.

His girls were.

His two special girls.

They were the centre of his world. The epicentre of his existence.

'Please leave,' he told the board. His voice was calm but he was anything but inside; tension was tying his muscles into such tight knots it felt as though he'd swallowed a ships anchor. 'I'll let you know when we'll reconvene.'

With much shuffling of paper and curious looks, the five men and two women picked up their belongings and made their way to the door.

As soon as they were alone, Alex rose to his feet and stalked across the room to Katrina. To give her her due, she didn't back away from him.

He stopped in front of her, so close they were

almost touching. He could smell the scent of her perfume and could see the little specks of golden-brown in cat-like green eyes that were focussed challengingly on him.

'Where have you been?' he demanded, resisting the urge to shake her until her teeth rattled.

Her chin angled upwards. 'Away.'

His hands clenched into fists. 'Away *where*?'

'It doesn't matter.'

Fury strung his flesh tightly together. 'It matters one hell of a damned lot when you take my daughter away without my permission and without telling me where you were going!'

She tossed her head, sending an invisible cloud of her scent into the air. 'I left you a note.'

He gritted his teeth. 'That's not good enough. Not by a long shot. Where is she?'

'She's right outside. Justine is looking after her.'

Relief washed through him, unravelling the tension that had hardened his insides.

'I could kill you for taking her,' he said.

'Is that why you announced to the world that Sam and I were missing?' she demanded, her eyes spitting chips of cold, green ice at him. 'I couldn't believe it when I saw our photos plastered all over the TV and newspapers.'

'Yes,' Alex hissed. 'You seem to be an expert at disappearing. I wasn't going to take the chance I'd never see my daughter again.'

She frowned. 'I told you in my note that I'd be in contact soon.'

'Forgive me, but *soon* just wasn't good enough.

Going to the press guaranteed me a result. The Royce Agency has already received floods of phone calls with possible sightings. If you hadn't turned up here this morning, it would only have been a matter of time before I tracked you down.'

She tossed her head again. 'Well, it worked. I came back. So, what do we do now?'

It was a good question.

Alex knew exactly what he wanted.

He just wasn't sure of his chances of getting it.

'That's entirely up to you. You either come back to me so that we provide Sam with the family she deserves, or we sort this out in court. Your choice.'

Alex imbued every word with as much determination as he could muster.

Samantha was Katrina's weak point. The threat of taking her daughter away from her had worked before. He was counting on it working again.

He could barely breathe as he waited for her answer.

Tension drew his shoulders up towards his ears and shrunk his stomach until it felt as though it had turned inside out.

The anger seemed to drain out of her. The eyes she turned on him were sad and filled with pain. 'I'm sorry, but I just can't do it. I can't sign up to a loveless relationship for the rest of my life.'

Her words were like an arrow piercing his heart. Although he was bleeding inside, Alex tried not to show it.

His mind grappled to find a solution, but there wasn't one.

If there was a way to make Katrina love him, then he

didn't know what it was. He wasn't a magician; he couldn't conjure something up out of thin air.

'I can't help you with that.' Alex could barely get the words out. 'You can't force feelings that just aren't there.'

Katrina flinched. Then she seemed to shrink in front of his eyes. Her shoulders sagged. Her head dropped. 'I can't. I'm sorry. My lawyer will be in contact with you to arrange joint custody. Goodbye, Alex.'

She turned on her heel and stalked to the door.

Something inside him twisted tight, so tight he expected it to snap.

'You can't leave,' he said in a voice he hardly recognised as his own.

But it was already too late. She'd gone.

Alex stared after her.

He couldn't breathe. He couldn't move. He couldn't even blink as her words penetrated deep into his soul.

An invisible hand gripped his heart.

His chest felt so tight he half-expected to hear his ribs crack under the pressure.

It couldn't be too late. It just couldn't. He wouldn't accept that it was over.

He loved her.

He'd been forced to admit the truth when he'd found her gone.

Gone. Katrina.

The words finally connected in his numbed brain.

She'd run out on him again!

With a curse, Alex sprang towards the door, yanked it open and began sprinting down the corridor towards the lift. Stabbing the down button, he barely contained his impatience until the door opened.

Every time the lift attempted to stop he pressed the closed button.

On the ground floor, Alex headed directly for David. He was only halfway across the vast foyer when the security guard spotted him and pointed upstairs.

Alex stopped then completed the distance more slowly, not sure if he was reading the guard's unspoken message correctly.

'She went back upstairs,' David said with a beaming smile. 'She got halfway across the foyer and then seemed to change her mind about leaving. Turned around and got straight back in the lift.'

His heart turned over, then did it again.

When she'd left he'd feared she'd given up.

On him. And them. And a future together.

Her return upstairs gave him a sliver of hope.

Alex thumped David on the back and grinned. 'Remind me to invite you to the wedding!'

'What do you mean, he's not here?' Katrina demanded. 'He was here two minutes ago.'

Justine nodded. 'I know. I think he went chasing after you.'

Her heart turned over in her chest. 'He did?'

Again, Justine nodded. 'Well, he ran out of here as if the building was on fire only a couple of minutes after you left.'

'Oh.'

Her heart flipped again. When Alex had let her walk away, she'd thought he'd given up.

On himself. On her. And on the possibility of them having a future together.

Surely the fact he'd gone chasing after her meant he hadn't given up?

The thought made her legs give way beneath her and she sank down on the visitor's chair on the opposite side of Justine's desk.

At that particular moment the door to Justine's office flew open. Without looking, Katrina knew who it was. She could sense Alex. It was as if his presence somehow changed the air particles between them, creating an invisible string that joined them together.

Katrina turned her head. Although she moved at normal speed, it felt as if she were moving in slow motion.

Alex stood in the doorway, staring at her with an odd look on his face.

Katrina stared back.

Neither said anything.

She sensed rather than saw Justine looking back and forth between them. After a moment, the other woman rose to her feet and cleared her throat. 'I think I'll give you guys some privacy.'

Katrina heard her but barely registered a word she said.

'You came back,' Alex breathed when the door closed.

Katrina nodded, hands clenched tightly together in her lap. 'I should never have left in the first place.'

She'd been halfway across the foyer before she'd realised that.

She'd been convinced that she couldn't live with Alex knowing that he didn't love her.

But saying goodbye had almost killed her.

She'd stopped in the middle of the vast foyer with tears stinging the back of her eyes.

And as she'd stood there she'd realised there was something worse—much, much worse—than living with the knowledge that Alex didn't love her. And that was being without him altogether.

She needed him whether he loved her or not.

His face was all planes and angles. 'Why not?'

'Because it's time I told you the truth.'

'And what truth is that?'

Katrina dragged in a deep breath for courage and flattened her spine against the back of the chair. Then she stared him straight in the eye. 'I love you.'

Alex gasped. 'Say that again.' His voice was strangled; his eyes locked on her face.

Undecided whether his reaction was good or bad, Katrina said it again.

Pleasure swept through him, bright and sweet.

Accepting Samantha into his life had enabled him to put the past behind him. As a result, he'd achieved the sort of peace he hadn't known existed. But the joy he felt now lifted his spirit, his soul, to another dimension.

A dimension where the light seemed brighter and the air smelled sweeter.

He smiled a big wide smile and watched Katrina blink.

Then he crossed the room in a couple of strides, grabbed her hands in his and pulled her to her feet, straight into his arms.

He didn't waste time talking. Instead, he claimed her mouth with his, telling her without words exactly how he felt about her.

Only when he knew they either had to stop or find somewhere more private did Alex lift his head. He rested his forehead against hers. 'You've made me the happiest man alive.'

'Have I?' she whispered.

He nodded and lifted his head so that he could look her in the eyes. He picked up her hands in his. 'Will you marry me?'

She tried to pull her hands away, but Alex wouldn't let her. She shook her head. 'No. I'll live with you, but I won't marry you.'

Alex frowned.

Had he misheard her a moment ago?

He was sure he'd heard Katrina say that she loved him. So what was the problem?

'Why not?' he demanded.

She shrugged. 'If I ever get married, it will be for the right reasons.'

Alex wondered if there was something wrong with the connection between his ears and his brain, because what Katrina was saying to him just didn't make sense. 'And what reasons would those be?'

If she wanted the moon, he would try to get it for her. The stars? No problem.

He would create miracles if that was what it took to have Katrina as his wife.

She angled her chin. 'Well, it certainly won't be because you feel obliged to do the right thing for our daughter.'

He cupped the side of her face. 'And is that the reason you think I asked?'

She nodded.

'Well, it's not.'

'Then why?'

He smiled, filling it with the intensity of the emotions teeming inside him. 'I asked because I love you.'

She gasped. 'No, you don't.'

'I do.' He smoothed the soft silkiness of her skin with his fingers. 'I think I've always loved you.'

She shook her head. 'I don't believe that!'

'Well, you should.' His mouth twisted. 'I seem to be very good at self-deception.'

She frowned. 'I don't understand.'

'Do you remember when you first came back? You burst into the board room like you did today.'

'What has—?'

He held up a hand. 'Wait. Let me finish. Do you remember I commented that you'd disappeared without a trace?'

She nodded. 'I remember. I made some crack about the TV show.'

'That's right. You did. I was glad you didn't give what I'd said too much thought, otherwise you might have realised what it meant.'

She frowned again, clearly puzzled. 'And what does it mean?'

Alex dragged in a breath. 'It means I had a private investigator searching for you. Not just in Sydney, but anywhere and everywhere.' He paused. 'I was desperate to find you.'

Her mouth twisted. 'That's only because I was pregnant.'

'Was it?' He recaptured her hands and squeezed them even more tightly. 'Don't forget, at the time I was convinced I wasn't the father.'

He felt her body jerk through their connecting hands as the importance of his words hit home.

'So, why were you looking for me then?' she asked, her voice little more than a whisper.

'That's the question, isn't it? I tried not to think about that too much. I didn't like the implication. I had all kinds of excuses, but the truth is that I was missing you like crazy.'

Her eyes glowed. 'Like crazy, huh? I like that.'

He pulled her to him and wrapped his arms around her waist. 'You do, do you?'

'Uh-huh.' Her face grew serious. 'You still don't have to marry me if you don't want to. Or have any more children.'

'I know I don't,' Alex replied with his usual arrogance. 'But I want the world to know that I love you and our daughter, and the best way to do that is to put a ring on your finger.' He put her away from him. 'And I *do* want more children.'

Her brow wrinkled. 'But you've arranged to have your vasectomy redone. Why would you do that if you want more children?'

Alex frowned and held her at arm's length. 'Who told you that?'

Katrina told him about the phone call from the doctor's office.

His frown cleared. 'I asked Dr Kershew to arrange the operation weeks ago,' Alex explained dismissively. 'It was just after I'd received the DNA test results. I was in a panic when I spoke to him. Maybe that's why he took so long to get back to me. To be honest, I'd completely forgotten I'd even mentioned it to him. Now that

I have my head straight, I'd love to have more children. A round dozen sounds like a good number.'

Katrina sputtered. 'I always said you were an over-achiever. Would you settle for half a dozen?'

His face grew serious. 'I'll settle for anything you want. I just want to make you happy. Do you know what I want to do right now?'

She shook her head.

'I want to take Sam and go home. I want to hold you both in my arms and tell you how much I love you. And then I want to take you to bed and start working on a brother or sister for her. What do you say?'

She took the hand he held out to her and squeezed it tight. And then she smiled. It was the most beautiful smile in the world. 'I'd like that. But I want you to know that, if all I ever have is you and Sam, I'll still be the happiest woman in the world.'

MILLS & BOON

APRIL 2010 HARDBACK TITLES

ROMANCE

The Italian Duke's Virgin Mistress	Penny Jordan
The Billionaire's Housekeeper Mistress	Emma Darcy
Brooding Billionaire, Impoverished Princess	Robyn Donald
The Greek Tycoon's Achilles Heel	Lucy Gordon
Ruthless Russian, Lost Innocence	Chantelle Shaw
Tamed: The Barbarian King	Jennie Lucas
Master of the Desert	Susan Stephens
Italian Marriage: In Name Only	Kathryn Ross
One-Night Pregnancy	Lindsay Armstrong
Her Secret, His Love-Child	Tina Duncan
Accidentally the Sheikh's Wife	Barbara McMahon
Marrying the Scarred Sheikh	Barbara McMahon
Tough to Tame	Diana Palmer
Her Lone Cowboy	Donna Alward
Millionaire Dad's SOS	Ally Blake
One Small Miracle	Melissa James
Emergency Doctor and Cinderella	Melanie Milburne
City Surgeon, Small Town Miracle	Marion Lennox

HISTORICAL

Practical Widow to Passionate Mistress	Louise Allen
Major Westhaven's Unwilling Ward	Emily Bascom
Her Banished Lord	Carol Townend

MEDICAL™

The Nurse's Brooding Boss	Laura Iding
Bachelor Dad, Girl Next Door	Sharon Archer
A Baby for the Flying Doctor	Lucy Clark
Nurse, Nanny...Bride!	Alison Roberts

0310 Gen Std LP

APRIL 2010 LARGE PRINT TITLES

ROMANCE

The Billionaire's Bride of Innocence	Miranda Lee
Dante: Claiming His Secret Love-Child	Sandra Marton
The Sheikh's Impatient Virgin	Kim Lawrence
His Forbidden Passion	Anne Mather
And the Bride Wore Red	Lucy Gordon
Her Desert Dream	Liz Fielding
Their Christmas Family Miracle	Caroline Anderson
Snowbound Bride-to-Be	Cara Colter

HISTORICAL

Compromised Miss	Anne O'Brien
The Wayward Governess	Joanna Fulford
Runaway Lady, Conquering Lord	Carol Townend

MEDICAL™

Italian Doctor, Dream Proposal	Margaret McDonagh
Wanted: A Father for her Twins	Emily Forbes
Bride on the Children's Ward	Lucy Clark
Marriage Reunited: Baby on the Way	Sharon Archer
The Rebel of Penhally Bay	Caroline Anderson
Marrying the Playboy Doctor	Laura Iding

MILLS & BOON

MAY 2010 HARDBACK TITLES

ROMANCE

Virgin on Her Wedding Night	Lynne Graham
Blackwolf's Redemption	Sandra Marton
The Shy Bride	Lucy Monroe
Penniless and Purchased	Julia James
Powerful Boss, Prim Miss Jones	Cathy Williams
Forbidden: The Sheikh's Virgin	Trish Morey
Secretary by Day, Mistress by Night	Maggie Cox
Greek Tycoon, Wayward Wife	Sabrina Philips
The French Aristocrat's Baby	Christina Hollis
Majesty, Mistress...Missing Heir	Caitlin Crews
Beauty and the Reclusive Prince	Raye Morgan
Executive: Expecting Tiny Twins	Barbara Hannay
A Wedding at Leopard Tree Lodge	Liz Fielding
Three Times A Bridesmaid...	Nicola Marsh
The No. 1 Sheriff in Texas	Patricia Thayer
The Cattleman, The Baby and Me	Michelle Douglas
The Surgeon's Miracle	Caroline Anderson
Dr Di Angelo's Baby Bombshell	Janice Lynn

HISTORICAL

The Earl's Runaway Bride	Sarah Mallory
The Wayward Debutante	Sarah Elliott
The Laird's Captive Wife	Joanna Fulford

MEDICAL™

Newborn Needs a Dad	Dianne Drake
His Motherless Little Twins	Dianne Drake
Wedding Bells for the Village Nurse	Abigail Gordon
Her Long-Lost Husband	Josie Metcalfe

0410 Gen Std LP

MAY 2010 LARGE PRINT TITLES

ROMANCE

Ruthless Magnate, Convenient Wife	Lynne Graham
The Prince's Chambermaid	Sharon Kendrick
The Virgin and His Majesty	Robyn Donald
Innocent Secretary...Accidentally Pregnant	Carol Marinelli
The Girl from Honeysuckle Farm	Jessica Steele
One Dance with the Cowboy	Donna Alward
The Daredevil Tycoon	Barbara McMahon
Hired: Sassy Assistant	Nina Harrington

HISTORICAL

Tall, Dark and Disreputable	Deb Marlowe
The Mistress of Hanover Square	Anne Herries
The Accidental Countess	Michelle Willingham

MEDICAL™

Country Midwife, Christmas Bride	Abigail Gordon
Greek Doctor: One Magical Christmas	Meredith Webber
Her Baby Out of the Blue	Alison Roberts
A Doctor, A Nurse: A Christmas Baby	Amy Andrews
Spanish Doctor, Pregnant Midwife	Anne Fraser
Expecting a Christmas Miracle	Laura Iding

millsandboon.co.uk Community

Join Us!

The Community is the perfect place to meet and chat to kindred spirits who love books and reading as much as you do, but it's also the place to:

- **Get the inside scoop from authors about their latest books**
- **Learn how to write a romance book with advice from our editors**
- **Help us to continue publishing the best in women's fiction**
- **Share your thoughts on the books we publish**
- **Befriend other users**

Forums: Interact with each other as well as authors, editors and a whole host of other users worldwide.

Blogs: Every registered community member has their own blog to tell the world what they're up to and what's on their mind.

Book Challenge: We're aiming to read 5,000 books and have joined forces with The Reading Agency in our inaugural Book Challenge.

Profile Page: Showcase yourself and keep a record of your recent community activity.

Social Networking: We've added buttons at the end of every post to share via digg, Facebook, Google, Yahoo, technorati and de.licio.us.

www.millsandboon.co.uk